Cherokee Myth and Legend

An Interpretation

by

Vernon Schmid

Copyright © 2006 by Vernon Schmid

All rights reserved. No part of this book shall be reproduced or transmitted in any form or by any means, electronic, mechanical, magnetic, photographic including photocopying, recording or by any information storage and retrieval system, without prior written permission of the publisher. No patent liability is assumed with respect to the use of the information contained herein. Although every precaution has been taken in the preparation of this book, the publisher and author assume no responsibility for errors or omissions. Neither is any liability assumed for damages resulting from the use of the information contained herein.

ISBN 0-7414-3499-7

Published by:

1094 New DeHaven Street, Suite 100
West Conshohocken, PA 19428-2713
Info@buybooksontheweb.com
www.buybooksontheweb.com
Toll-free (877) BUY BOOK
Local Phone (610) 941-9999
Fax (610) 941-9959

Printed in the United States of America

Printed on Recycled Paper

Published August 2006

Also by Vernon Schmid

Between Eleven and Thursday
One Night in Daylight
The Hare with Many Friends
Poets and Priests and Madmen
Pilgrims
The Irish Poems
Northern Ireland:
War and Peace in the Land of Saints and Scholars
Media and Methods for Your Church
The Desert and the Dance
Of the Heart and the Bread (editor)
The Journey Toward
As Tentative as Flight (co-author)
Canonical Hours
Five Who Knew Jesus
Testament
Sleeping with Zapata
Hog Killers and Other Poems
Seven Days of the Dog
Kissing Moctezuma's Serpent
Houlihans and Horse Sense
Showdown at Chalk Creek
Westering: New and Selected Poems, 1974-2004
Otium Sanctum: Poems for the Journey Toward
Jacob's War

Contents

Creation
How We Came to Be	3
Buzzard Shapes the World	4
The Seventh Height	5
The Underworld	6
In the Beginning	7
Fire	8
First Family	10
The Deluge	19

Serpents
Thunder's Necklace	23
The Great Serpent	25
Rattlesnake's Vengeance	28
Odds and Ends	30
Copperhead	30
Blacksnake	30
Greensnake	30
Spreading Adder	31

Birds of a Feather
Attack of the Birds	35
How They Brought Back the Tobacco	37
The Hunter and the Hawk	39
Eagle	41
Owl	44
Buzzard the Physician	45
Hummingbird and Crane in Love	46
Mudhen	48
Turkey's Neck	49
How Turkey Got His Gobble	50
Bird Calls	51
The Great Mythic Hawk	52
Why Owl is Skinny	54
Why Buzzard's Head is Bare	56
How Kingfisher Got His Bill	57
How Partridge Got His Whistle	58

How Redbird Got His Color	59
Eagle's Revenge	60

Immortals, Spirits and Monsters

The People Who Live Anywhere	63
The Boy and the Immortals	64
Water Cannibals	66
The Prosperous Trader	67
Immortal Women Come to Dance	69
Immortal Voices	70
Fish and Frogs	72
Bear Man	73
Spear Finger	77
Stone Man	81
Burnt-Tobacco and the Immortals	84
Fire under the Mountain	85
Townhouse of the Immortals	86
Where They Cried	87
The Slant-Eyed Giant	89
The Lost Settlement	95
Immortals as Protectors	98
A Race of Spirits	99
The Cave	100
The Hunter and the Great Fish	101
Enchanted Lake	102
Ice Man	103
The Hunter and Corn	105
The Handsome Fairy	106
Fire Carrier	107
Raven Mocker	108
The Young Man and The Raven Mockers	110
The Rescue	112
Water Dwellers	113
Friendly Spirits	114
The Sick Man	115
Mischievous Spirits	117

Sun, Moon and Stars

The Boys	121
Where the Dog Ran	122
Stars	123
Frog Swallows the Sun	124

Animal Tales

Rabbit and Terrapin Race	127
Rabbit Loses His Tail	129
Rabbit Hunts Duck	131
Rabbit and the Tar Wolf	133
Rabbit and Bear Dine Together	134
Rabbit and Possum Seek Wives	135
Rabbit and Flint	137
Rabbit and Wildcat Hunt Turkeys	139
Why Possum's Tail is Bare	141
Tadpole Lover	143
Bullfrog Lover	144
Why Bullfrog's Head is Striped	145
Deer Gets Antlers	146
Terrapin Escapes	147
Katydid's Warning	149
Origin of the Bear	150
Why Mink Stinks	152
Why Groundhog's Tail is Short	153
Dog and Wolf	155
Why Deer's Teeth Are Blunt	156
Deer's Revenge	158

Thunder and Lightning

Thunder and His Sons	161
The Man Who Loved Thunder's Sister	162
Thunder's Child	166
Red Man	172
The Rescue of Red Man	173

The Cherokee Rose and Other Stories

The Cherokee Rose	177
The Suck	178
Man in the Stump	179
Strawberries	180
Two Old Men	181
The Lazy Hunter	182
Hearts Forever Broken	184
When Babies are Born	185

Dedication

This volume is dedicated to the memory of the Cherokee "Old Settlers" in Arkansas, sometimes called the Chickamauga or the Western Cherokees, one of which was Onicyphorus Standlee, my great-great-great grandfather whose Cherokee mother married an Englishman in the Carolina Mountains in the eighteenth century.

Foreword

Joseph Campbell said, "The common tendency today to read the word "myth" as meaning "untruth" is almost certainly a symptom of the incredibility and consequent inefficacy of our own outdated mythic teachings, both of the Old Testament and of the New; the Fall of Adam and Eve, Tablets of Law, Fires of Hell, Second Coming of the Savior, etc.; and not only of archaic religious Testaments but also of the various modern, secular Utopiates." He further stated, "Myths are clues to unite the forces within us."

In other words, myth makes the connection between waking consciousness and universal mysteries, our relationship with all creation. It is so with every tradition in the world. Like all such traditions, the stories handed down from one generation to another over millennia serve as an experiential basis of existence for all people, all religions, and all cultures.

To begin to understand myth and legend it is necessary to put aside individual mythologies and let the ancient world of a specific people take over.

In Cherokee mythology and legend there is no essential difference between human beings and animals. From the beginning, all creatures lived and worked together in harmony until the two-leggeds, through aggressiveness and disregard for the rights of the others, provoked the hostility of the four-leggeds, insects, birds, fish and reptiles. Since that time, it is said, they have been separate.

The difference between them is only a matter of degree. Animals, like the Real People, are organized into tribes and have chiefs, townhouses, councils and ballgames. At the end of their life they also go to the same Darkening Land.

Two-leggeds, of course, are the most powerful. They hunt and kill at will. Nevertheless, they are obliged to satisfy animal tribes in every instance. Therefore, pardon is available to the hunter, partly, because of a doctrine of reincarnation. According to legend there is assigned to every living creature a definite life term, which cannot be curtailed by violent means. If killed before the end of the allotted time, the body is resurrected in its proper shape from blood drops. The animal then continues its existence until the end of the predestined period. Then, the spirit is free to join its kindred in the Darkening Land.

Supernatural personages have dominion over animals. Some are gods of the hunter. Primeval animals and their predecessors were larger, stronger, and cleverer than their descendants who live today. In the stories that follow, the reader will find explanations of form, color, habit and how various animals act in accordance with their particular characteristics.

My own Cherokee ancestors lived in the Smoky Mountains until they became part of a group known as the Old Settlers moving west before the New Echota Treaty and the Removal. Their journey took them from North Carolina through Tennessee and Kentucky and ultimately to the Ozark Mountains of Arkansas. Today their descendants live all over that region and far beyond.

As I encountered, collected and began to retell these stories, I imagined my ancestors sitting in an old rocking chair of twisted grape vine, gray with time, telling me the stories.

Gathered from many places and times over the years, some told to me, others gleaned from books and other sources, they have long gathered dust in my library and files. I now attempt to recast them and tell them anew as all storytellers do. However, the stories still belong to the *Tsalagi*, the Real People.

I hope my attempt at these interpretations conveys the wonder of how people come to know who they are and how they came to be. If there is error, it is mine alone and unintentional and I pray my brothers and sisters may forgive.

– Vernon Schmid

Creation

How We Came to Be

In time before time, before the Real People emerged, animals huddled in fear beyond a great stone vaulted sky separated from a vast fearful world of blue water far below.

Knees banged against knees, elbows jabbed against elbows, wings beat against wings. They dreamed of freedom, freedom to stretch their wings, freedom to dance.

And yet, none was brave enough to leave the stone vaulted sky's protection, until Beaver's tiny grandchild, Little Water Beetle, stepped forward, head respectfully bowed, offering to go explore below.

Council knew her courage. Therefore, they sent her to the frightening unknown water world, where she skated on the blue surface, as she does even to this day.

However, she did not discover a place for animals. Then insight, perhaps, or the Great Mystery possessed her. She dove deep into the sea finding mud to be gathered and spread on water where new land became what some call earth, others call Turtle Island.

It is held firmly to the sky by four strong cords. One at each corner of the world. However, when the world is old and worn the cords will break. Turtle Island will sink. All will die. It is this the Real People fear.

Buzzard Shapes the World

Council sent Great Buzzard, father of all buzzards, to fly over this new land seeking a place for animals to settle. He flew until his exhausted wings grew tired and flapped downward against wet new earth causing green valleys to appear. His wings then turned up shaping blue smoking mountains.

Fearing the entire world would be mountains, Council called him home. And still, the Real People love blue mountains and deep green valleys.

The Seventh Height

In the cold, dark new world Conjurers sent Sun across the island, traveling east to west as it was meant to be.

It was so close to the earth the Real People were burned brown. It scorched Crayfish's thin shell bright red spoiling the meat. Therefore, Cherokees do not eat crayfish to this day.

Conjurers then set Sun a handbreadth higher. Still, it was too hot. They raised it again and again until it was seven handbreadths high under the great sky vault.

They gazed on their work and left Sun there, naming it "The Seventh Height."

Now, every day Sun travels under the arch, returning at night to its starting place, to begin another cycle, providing light, keeping the Real People warm, telling corn to grow.

The Underworld

Beneath this world, an underworld exists. It has animals, plants, and people. Only the seasons differ.

Water warms in winter, cools in summer. Streams are trails to the underworld. Springs are doorways by which the Real People may enter with underworld spirits as guides.

In the Beginning

When animals and plants were made, we do not know by whom, they were told, "Watch, fast, keep awake for seven nights, as young men fast, keeping awake, praying for their vision."

All tried to do this. Nearly all were awake through the first night. The next night several fell asleep. On the third night others fell asleep.

On the seventh night, only Owl, Panther, and few others remained awake. To these were given the power to see in the dark and prey on birds and animals sleeping at night.

Of the trees, only Cedar, Pine, Spruce, Holly and Laurel were awake to the end. They would always be green and be great for medicine.

To other trees it was said, "Because you have not endured you shall lose your hair every winter."

Fire

In the beginning, there was no fire. The world was cold.

Thunder sent Lightning, his son, to put Fire in a hollow Sycamore on an island.

The animals knew Fire was there. They could see smoke coming out of the top of the Sycamore, however, they could not reach it because water surrounded the island.

Anxious to get fire, Raven volunteered. Large and strong, Council thought he could do it. Raven flew across the water lighting on the Sycamore. Fire scorched him black. Frightened, he returned without Fire.

Little Screech Owl volunteered. As he looked into the hollow tree hot air blasted up nearly burning out his eyes. They are red to this day.

Hooting Owl and Horned Owl went together. Fire burned fiercely, smoke nearly blinded them. Ashes carried by the wind made white rings around their eyes that remain to this day. After that, no more birds ventured out.

Little Black Racer offered to bring back Fire. Swimming to the island, he crawled through grass to the tree and entered a hole at the bottom. Heat and smoke overwhelmed him. Dodging blindly over the hot ashes, nearly on fire, he escaped but was scorched black. Even today, he darts about trying to escape.

Great Blacksnake, the climber, then volunteered. He swam to the island, climbed the tree, put his head in the hole. Smoke choked him. He fell into the stump burned black before escaping.

Still they had no Fire. The world remained cold.

Council met again seeking volunteers. However, birds, snakes, and all four-footeds, were afraid.

Finally, Water Spider said she would go. This is not the water spider resembling a mosquito. It is the black downy one with red stripes on her body. She runs on top of water, dives to the bottom. Getting to the island would be easy for her.

The question was, "How could she bring back Fire?"

So, Water Spider spun a thread from her body, wove it into a *tusti,* a bowl, and fastened it to her back. She swam to the island, crawled through grass to where Fire was burning. She put one little coal in her bowl and brought it back so we have Fire.

Today Water Spider keeps the *tusti*, she keeps her bowl.

First Family

First man, *Kana'ti*, Lucky Hunter, and his wife, *Selu*, Corn, had one son they called Only Child.

Lucky Hunter always found game. Corn prepared it, washing it in the nearby river. Only Child played by the river every day.

Hearing laughter in the bushes near the river, the parents thought it sounded like children playing. They asked Only Child who was playing with him.

The boy shrugged saying, "He comes out of the water. He calls himself my brother. He says his mother was cruel throwing him into the river."

Then the parents knew the strange boy sprang from the blood of the game Corn washed at river's edge.

When Only Child went out to play the other boy joined him, but he always went back into the water. The parents never saw their son's playmate.

Lucky Hunter said to his son, "Tomorrow, when Wild Boy comes to play, wrestle with him. When you have your arms around him, hold him, call for us."

Only Child promised to do so.

The next day when Wild Boy appeared, Only Child challenged him to a wrestling match. When their arms were locked around each other, Lucky Hunter's son began screaming. His parents came running.

When Wild Boy saw them, he struggled to be free, crying, "Let me go. You threw me away!"

Only Child held on until his parents reached them. They seized Wild Boy and took him home. They called him, "He-who-grew-up-wild."

They kept him in the house and tamed him, but he remained wild and artful. He always led his brother in mischief. It was not long until the parents discovered he had magic powers.

***

One day Wild Boy said, "I wonder where our father gets all that game? Let's follow him and find out."

A few days afterward, Lucky Hunter took his bow and arrows and started west. The boys followed him, keeping out of sight and watched him go into a swamp.

Wild Boy changed himself into a puff of bird's down, which the wind carried onto Lucky Hunter's shoulder as he entered the swamp unaware.

When Luck Hunter left the swamp to climb the mountain, the wind blew the down from his shoulder. It fell in the woods.

Wild Boy took his original shape.

Then the boys followed him up the mountain, where he stopped to lift a rock from the mouth of a cave. When he did a buck deer ran out. Lucky Hunter shot it, lifted it up onto his back and started home.

The boys exclaimed, "Oho! He keeps all the deer shut up in that hole. Whenever he wants meat he just lets one out to kill."

They hurried home before their father so he would not know they followed him.

A few days later, the boys went back to the swamp, cut reeds, made seven arrows and started up the mountain to where their father kept the game. When they got to the place, they raised the rock. A deer ran out. As they drew back to shoot it, another came out, then another and another. The boys, confused, forgot why they were there.

In those days, deer tails hung down like other animals. As a buck ran past, Wild Boy struck its tail with an arrow. It pointed upward. The boys thought this good sport. When the next one ran past Wild Boy struck its tail. It too stood straight up. His brother struck the next one so hard the deer's tail almost curled over his back. Deer carries his tail this way ever since. The deer ran by until the last one came out of the hole, escaping into the forest.

Raccoons, rabbits, all four-footed animals, except

Bear, came out of the cave. There was no bear then. Last came flocks of turkeys, pigeons, partridges darkening the air like a cloud, making a great noise.

Sitting at home, Lucky Hunter heard a sound like thunder on the mountain and said to himself, "My boys are in trouble. I must go and see what they are doing."

He went up the mountain to the place where he kept the game finding the two boys standing by the rock. All the birds and animals were gone. Lucky Hunter was furious.

He went to the cave, kicked the covers off four jars. Out swarmed bedbugs, fleas, lice, gnats. They landed on the boys. The boys screamed with pain and fright, trying to beat off the insects, but thousands crawled over them, bit and stung them until both nearly died. Lucky Hunter watched all of this until he thought they were punished enough.

Then he said, "Now, you rascals, you have always had plenty to eat and never had to work for it. Whenever you were hungry, all I had to do was come, get a deer or a turkey, and bring it home for your mother to cook. However, you let out all the animals. After this when you want a deer to eat you will have to hunt the woods for it and maybe not find one. Go home to your mother, while I see if I can find something to eat for supper."

***

When the boys got home, they were tired and hungry. They asked their mother for something to eat.

Corn said, "There is no meat, but I'll get you something."

She took a basket to the storehouse. The storehouse was on poles high up from the ground to keep it out of the reach of animals. There was a ladder to climb up and one door, but no other opening. Every day when Corn got ready to cook, she would go to the storehouse with a basket and bring it back full of corn and beans.

The boys had never been inside the storehouse. They

wondered from where all the corn and beans came since the storehouse was not a very large one.

As soon as Corn went out the door, Wild Boy said to his brother, "Let's go see what she does."

They climbed up one of the poles and pulled a piece of clay from between the logs so they could see inside. They saw their mother standing in the middle of the room, a basket in front of her on the floor. Leaning over the basket, she rubbed her stomach. The basket half-filled with corn. She rubbed her armpits. The basket filled with beans.

The boys said, "Our mother is a witch. If we eat this food it will poison us. We must kill her."

When the boys came back into the house, she knew their thoughts before they spoke.

She said, "So you are going to kill me?"

The boys said, "Yes, you are a witch."

Corn said, "Well, when you kill me, clear a large piece of ground in front of the house. Drag my body seven times around the circle. Then drag me seven times over the ground inside the circle. Stay up all night and watch. In the morning you will have plenty of corn."

The boys killed her with clubs, cut off her head, put it on the roof of the house, her face turned to the west, to look for her husband.

They cleared the ground in front of the house. Instead of clearing it all, they cleared only seven little spots. This is why corn grows in only a few places instead of over the whole world.

They dragged their mother's body around the circle. Wherever her blood fell, corn sprang up. Instead of dragging her body seven times across the ground as she instructed, they dragged it twice. Therefore, Indians work their crop only twice. The two brothers watched the corn all night. In the morning, it was grown and ripe.

***

When Lucky Hunter came home, he did not see his wife. He asked the boys where their mother was.

They said, "She was a witch. So, we killed her. There is her head on top of the house."

Seeing his wife's head on the roof, Lucky Hunter became angry saying, "I won't stay with you any longer. I am going to the wolf people."

Before he had gone far Wild Boy changed himself again to a tuft of down and lighted on Lucky Hunter's shoulder. When Lucky Hunter reached the settlement of the wolf people, they were holding council. He went in and sat down.

When the wolf chief asked him his business, he said, "I have two bad boys. I want you to go in seven days and play ball against them."

The wolves knew he meant for them to kill the boys.

The bird's down blew off Lucky Hunter's shoulder. The smoke carried it up through the hole in the council house roof. When it came down outside, Wild Boy took his right shape, went home and told his brother what he had heard in the council.

The boys got ready for the wolves. Wild Boy and his brother ran around the house in a wide circle until they made a trail all around it except the side from which the Wolves would come. There they left a small open space. They made four large bundles of arrows, placed them at four different points of the circle, and hid in the woods waiting for the wolves.

Within a few days, a party of wolves came and surrounded the house to kill the boys. The wolves did not notice the trail around the house, because they came in where the boys had left the opening. Once inside the circle it changed to a high brush fence shutting them in, while the boys began shooting the trapped. They were nearly all killed. Only a few escaped into a great swamp close by. The boys ran around the swamp and a circle of fire sprang up in their tracks, setting fire to grass and bushes, burning up nearly all the wolves. Only two or three survived. From these come all the wolves now in the world.

***

Strangers came to ask the boys for some grain. The boys gave them seven grains of corn telling them to plant the next night on their way home, watching the corn all night, then they would have seven ripe ears in the morning.

The strangers took the seven grains, watched all through the night. In the morning they saw seven tall stalks, each bearing a ripened ear. They gathered the ears and went on their way.

The next night they planted all their corn, guarding it as before until daybreak, when they found abundant increase.

However, their journey was long, the sun was hot, and the people grew tired. On the last night before reaching home, they fell asleep. In the morning, the corn they planted had not sprouted.

They brought with them to their settlement the corn they had left and planted it with care and attention to raise a crop.

Ever since that time corn must be watched and tended through half the year unlike before when it would grow and ripen overnight.

***

Meanwhile, leaving the Wolf People Lucky Hunter did not return home. He went farther away. The boys decided to find him.

Wild Boy took a gaming wheel and rolled it toward the Darkening land. In a little while, the wheel came rolling back. The boys knew their father was not there.

Then Wild Boy rolled it south, then north, each time the wheel came back to him. They knew their father was not there.

Then Wild Boy rolled it toward Sunland. It did not

return.

Wild Boy said, "Our father is there, let us go and find him."

The brothers set off toward the east. After traveling a long time they came upon Lucky Hunter walking along with a dog by his side.

Lucky Hunter said, "You bad boys, why have you come here?"

They answered, "We always accomplish what we start out to do. We are now men."

Lucky Hunter said, "This dog overtook me four days ago."

The boys knew the dog was the wheel, sent to find him.

Lucky Hunter said, "As you have found me, we may as well travel together, but I shall take the lead."

Soon they came to a swamp. Lucky Hunter told them there was something dangerous there, and they must keep away from it. He went on ahead of the boys.

As soon as he was out of sight, Wild Boy said to his brother, "Come. Let's see what is in the swamp."

They went into the middle of the swamp. There a large panther was sleeping. Wild Boy shot the panther with an arrow on one side of the head. The panther turned his head and the other boy shot him on that side. He turned his head away and the brothers shot together *tust, tust, tust!* The panther was not hurt by the arrows. It paid no attention to the boys.

Then the boys left the swamp overtaking Lucky Hunter who was waiting for them.

He asked, "Did you find it?"

The boys said, "Yes, we found it, but it never hurt us. We are men."

Lucky Hunter was surprised, but he said nothing.

They traveled on. After a while, he turned to them and said, "Now you must be careful. We are coming to a tribe called the *Anäda'dûñtäskï*. They are cannibals. If they get you they will feast on you."

Soon the boys came to a lightning struck tree. Wild Boy directed his brother to gather some splinters from the tree. In a little while, they came to the settlement of the cannibals, who saw the boys and came running out, crying, "Good, here are two nice fat strangers. We'll have a grand feast!"

They caught the boys, dragged them into the townhouse and sent word to all the people to come feast. They made a great fire, put water into a large pot, set it to boiling and placed Wild Boy in the pot. His brother, did not attempt to escape. He knelt down and began putting the splinters into the fire, as if to make it burn better. When the cannibals thought the meat was about ready they lifted the pot from the fire.

At that instant, a blinding light filled the townhouse. Lightning darted from one side to the other, striking down cannibals until all were dead. Then Lightning went up through the smoke hole. The next moment the two boys were standing outside the townhouse as though nothing had happened.

***

The two boys went on and again met Lucky Hunter who seemed surprised to see them.

He said, "What! Are you here again?"

The boys replied, "O, yes, we never give up. We are great men!"

Their father asked, "What did the cannibals do to you?"

The boys explained, "We met them. They brought us to their townhouse. But, they never hurt us."

Lucky Hunter was silent as he traveled out of sight of the boys, who kept on until they came to the end of the world, where the sun comes out.

***

The sky was coming down. When it went up again. The boys went through climbing up on the other side. There they found Lucky Hunter and Corn sitting together. Their parents received them kindly and were glad to see them, telling them they might stay a while but then they must go to live where the sun goes down.

The boys stayed seven days before going on to the Darkening Land, where they are today. We call them *Anisga'ya Tsunsdi'*, the Little Men. When they talk to each other, we hear low rolling thunder in the west.

***

It is also said that after Lucky Hunter's boys let the deer out of the cave, hunters tramped the woods for a long time without finding any game so the Real People were very hungry. At last, they heard the Thunder Boys were living in the far west, beyond the sun door and that if they were sent for they could bring back the game. Messengers went to them.

The boys sat in the middle of the townhouse and began to sing. With the first song, a roaring sound like a strong wind came from the northwest, growing louder and nearer. The boys sang on until the seventh song when a herd of deer, led by a large buck, came out of the woods. With bows and arrows the People were ready when the song ended. The deer were close. The hunters shot. Killing as many as needed.

The Thunder Boys went back to the Darkening Land, but before leaving, they taught the people seven songs with which to call up the deer.

All but two of the songs are forgotten, which hunters still sing whenever they go after deer.

The Deluge

A man and his dog loved the river. Each day the dog looked at the water and howled. The angry man scolded the dog.

The dog spoke to him saying, "Very soon there is going to be a great freshet. The water will come so high everybody will drown; but if you will make a raft to get upon when the rain comes, you can be saved, but first you must throw me into the water."

The man did not believe.

The dog said, "If you want a sign that I speak the truth, look at the back of my neck."

The man looked. He saw the dog's neck had the skin worn off so bones stuck out. He believed the dog and began to build a raft. Soon the rain came, he took his family, and plenty of provisions. They got on the raft. The water rose until the mountains were covered and all the people in the world drowned.

Then the rain stopped. The waters went down until it was safe to come off the raft. There was no one alive but the man and his family. They heard dancing and shouting on the other side of a ridge. The man climbed to the top to look over.

Everything was still, but all along the valley he saw great piles of bones of the people who had drowned and he knew ghosts had been dancing.

Serpents

Thunder's Necklace

Once a man, Rattlesnake, *Utsa'nããtïï*, is sometimes called "He has a bell" or "Thunder's necklace."

Rattlesnake transformed to save two-leggeds from extermination by the Sun. His mission was accomplished after others failed. To kill one is to destroy Thunder God's prized ornament.

The Little Men, sons of Thunder, are implored to take the snake to themselves as adornments.

Feared and respected, few Cherokees venture to kill Rattlesnake unless necessary. Even then, the crime must be atoned for by asking pardon of the snake ghost, either in person or through the mediation of a shaman. Otherwise, relatives of the dead snake track the offender and bite him so he will die.

***

Rattlesnake fears campion, used by the doctors to counteract the effect of the bite. It is believed that a snake will flee in terror from the hunter carrying the root about his person.

Notwithstanding fear of Rattlesnake, his rattles, teeth, flesh, and oil are prized for occult or medical uses. They are killed for this purpose by certain medicine men who know the necessary rites and formulas for obtaining pardon.

Outsiders desiring this knowledge are discouraged by being told it is a dangerous thing to learn. The new initiate is almost certain to be bitten so the snakes may "try" him to know if he has correctly learned the formula.

When Rattlesnake is killed, the head must be cut off and buried an arm's length deep in the ground and the body carefully hidden in a hollow log. If it is left exposed to weather, angry snakes send torrents of rain to overflow streams.

Moreover, they tell their friends, Deer and Ginseng in the mountains, so that they hide themselves and hunters seek them in vain.

The tooth of Rattlesnake killed by a shaman with proper ceremonies while the snake was lying stretched out from east to west is used to scarify patients preliminary to applying the medicine in certain ailments. Before using it the doctor holds it between thumb and finger addressing it in prayer, at the end of which the tooth comes alive, when it is ready for the operation. The explanation is that the tense, nervous grasp of the doctor causes his hand to twitch and the tooth to move between his fingers.

Rattles are worn on the head and sometimes ball players, to make them more terrible to their opponents eat a portion of the flesh but it is said to have a bad effect of making them cross with their wives.

From the lower half of the body, thought to be the fattest portion, oil is extracted. It is in great repute among Indians for rheumatism and sore joints as among mountaineers. The doctor preparing the oil must also eat the flesh of the snake.

In certain seasons of epidemic, a roasted rattlesnake is kept hanging in the house. Every morning the father of the family bites off a small piece, chews it, mixes it with water, which he spits upon the bodies of the others preserving them from the contagion. It is said to be a sure cure, but apt to make patients hot tempered.

The Great Serpent

The great serpent *Ustûû'tlïï*, haunted Cohutta Mountain.

Unlike other snakes, it had feet at each end of its body, moving by strides and jerks, like a great measuring worm. The feet were three-cornered and flat holding on to the ground like suckers.

It had no legs, but could raise itself up on its hind feet, its snaky head waving high in the air until it found a good place to take a fresh hold. It would then bend down, grip its front feet to the ground, drawing its body up from behind.

It could cross-rivers and deep ravines by throwing its head across, getting a grip with its front feet and swinging its body over.

Wherever its footprints were found there was danger.

It used to bleat like a young fawn.

When a hunter heard a fawn bleat in the woods, he never looked for it, but hurried away in the other direction.

Up the mountain or down, nothing could escape *Ustûû'tlïï's* pursuit. However, along the side of the ridge it could not go, because the great weight of its swinging head broke its hold on the ground when it moved sideways.

And so it came to be that not a hunter would venture near the mountain for dread of *Ustûû'tlïï*.

***

A man from a northern settlement came visiting relatives in the settlement. When he arrived, they made a feast for him, but had only corn and beans. They excused themselves for having no meat because the hunters were afraid to go to the mountains.

He asked the reason and they told him. He said he

would go himself and either bring in a deer or find *Ustûû'tliï.*

The People warned that if he heard a fawn bleat in the thicket he must run at once. If the snake came after him, they said, he must not try to run down the mountain. He must run along the ridge.

In the morning, he went to the mountain. Working his way through the bushes, he heard the bleat of a fawn. He knew it was *Ustûû'tliï*.

He made up his mind to see it, therefore he did not turn back. He went straight toward the sound.

The monster raised its great head in the air as high as the pine branches, looking in every direction to discover a deer, or maybe a man, for breakfast.

It saw the hunter and came at him moving in jerky strides, every one the length of a tree trunk, holding its scaly head high above the bushes, bleating as it came.

The hunter was so frightened he lost his wits and started to run directly up the mountain.

The great snake came after him, gaining half its length every time it took a fresh grip with its fore feet.

It would have caught the hunter before he reached the mountaintop but the hunter suddenly remembered the warning. He changed his course, ran along the sides of the mountain. At once, the snake began to lose ground.

Every time it raised itself up the weight of its body threw it out of a straight line making it fall a little lower down the side of the ridge. It tried to recover, but the hunter was gaining.

He kept running until he turned the end of the ridge leaving the snake out of sight. There he cautiously climbed to the top, looked over and saw *Ustûû'tliï* slowly working its way toward the summit.

He went down to the base of the mountain, opened his fire pouch, set fire to the grass and leaves. Soon fire ran all around the mountain climbing upward. When the great snake smelled the smoke and saw the flames coming, it forgot all about the hunter.

Turning, it raced for a high cliff near the summit,

reached a rock and got upon it but the fire followed, burned the dead pines at the base of the cliff until the heat made *Ustûû'tlïï's* scales crack.

Gripping the rock with its hind feet it raised its body putting forth all its strength to spring across the wall of fire surrounding it, but the smoke choked it, its hold loosened, it fell among blazing pine trunks, laying there until it was burned to ashes.

Rattlesnake's Vengeance

In the old times, children were playing about the house when their mother heard them scream.

Running out she found a rattlesnake, took up a stick and killed it.

The father was hunting in the mountains and that evening coming home after dark through the gap he heard a strange wailing sound. Looking about he found he had was in the midst of a whole company of rattlesnakes; all had their mouths open and seemed to be crying.

He asked them the reason of their trouble. They told him his wife killed their chief, Yellow Rattlesnake. They were about to send Black Rattlesnake to take revenge.

The hunter apologized, but they told him if he spoke the truth he must be ready to make satisfaction giving his wife as sacrifice for the life of their chief. Not knowing what might happen otherwise, he consented.

They then told him Black Rattlesnake would go home with him, coil up just outside the door in the dark. He must go inside to ask his wife to go get him a drink of fresh water from the spring. That was all.

He went home knowing Black Rattlesnake was following.

It was night when he arrived and very dark, but he found his wife waiting with his supper ready. He sat down and asked for a drink of water. She handed him a gourd full from a jar.

He said he wanted it fresh from the spring. So, she took a bowl and went out of the door.

The next moment he heard a cry and going out he found Black Rattlesnake had bitten her and she was dying.

He stayed with her until she was dead. Then, Black Rattlesnake came out of the grass and said his tribe was now satisfied.

He taught the hunter a prayer song saying, "When you meet any of us hereafter sing this song and we will not hurt you; but if by accident one of us should bite one of your people sing this song over him and he will recover."

The Real People keep the song to this day.

Odds and Ends

Copperhead

Wââ'dige-askââ'lïï, Copperhead, feared for its poisonous bite, hated instead of being venerated like Rattlesnake, is believed to be a descendant of a great mythic serpent with eyes for fire.

***

Blacksnake

Blacksnake, *Gûûle'gïi*, "the climber" prevents toothache if you bite its body.
 If the body of one is hung upon a tree it will bring rain within three or four days.
 They are also known to be good for farmers since they live in the barn feasting upon rodents, leaving the shed skin for decoration.

***

Greensnake

Greensnake, *Säälikwââ'yïi*, is named for bear grass, whose long, slender leaves resemble Greensnake.
 Like Blacksnake, it is believed toothache may be prevented and sound teeth insured as long as life lasts by biting Greensnake along its body.

This is how it must be done. The head and tail must be held with all teeth pressed down four times along the middle of its body without biting into the flesh or injuring the snake.

It must be repeated four times upon four snakes and certain foods must be avoided.

***

Spreading Adder

The spreading adder, *Daliïkstää'*, called the vomiter because it spits, is repulsive but harmless.

Adder was formerly a man, but was transformed into a snake to accomplish the destruction of Sun's daughter.

For its failure, it is generally despised.

Birds of a Feather

Attack of the Birds

Once young warriors set out to see what was in the world. They traveled south until they came to a tribe of little people called *Tsundige'wï*.

They were hardly tall enough to reach a man's knee. They had no houses. They lived in nests scooped in the sand and covered with dried grass. The little people were so weak they could not fight and were in constant terror from the wild geese and other birds that used to come in great flocks from the south to make war upon them.

Just at the time the travelers got there they found the little people in great fear, because there was a strong wind blowing from the south carrying white feathers down along the sand. The *Tsundige'wï* knew their enemies were not far behind. The young warriors asked them why they did not defend themselves.

They said they could not because they did not know how. There was no time to make bows and arrows. So, the travelers told them to take sticks for clubs and showed them where to strike the birds to kill them.

The wind blew for days. At last, the birds came. There were so many they were like a great cloud in the air. The little people ran to their nests, the birds following to stick in their long bills to pull the little people out and eat them.

This time though, the *Tsundige'wï* had clubs. They struck the birds on the neck as the young warriors had shown them. They killed so many that at last the other birds were glad to spread their wings and fly away again to the south.

The little people thanked the young warriors for their help and gave them the best they had until the travelers went on to other tribes.

Afterwards they heard that the birds came again several times, but the *Tsundige'wï* always drove them off with their clubs until a flock of Sandhill Cranes came. They were so tall the little people could not reach up to strike them on the neck and so at last, the cranes killed them all.

How They Brought Back the Tobacco

In the beginning of the world, when people and animals were all the same, there was only one tobacco plant to which all came for their tobacco.

One day *Dagûl`kû* the geese stole it carrying it far away to the south and the people suffered.

An old woman grew thin and weak. Every one said she would soon die unless she could get tobacco to keep her alive.

Different animals offered to go for it.

One after another, the larger ones first, then the smaller ones, but the *Dagûl`kû* saw and killed every one before they could get to the plant.

After the others, Mole tried to reach it going under the ground, but the *Dagûl`kû* saw his track and killed him as he came out.

At last, Hummingbird offered.

The others said he was too small and might as well stay at home. He begged them to let him try, so they showed him a plant in a field telling him to let them see how he would go about it.

The next moment he was gone.

They saw him sitting on the plant. In a moment, he was back again, but no one had seen him going or coming because he was so swift.

Hummingbird said, "This is the way I'll do it."

He flew to the east. When he came in sight of the tobacco the *Dagûl`kû* were watching all about it. They could not see him because he was so small and flew so swiftly. He darted down on the plant—*tsa!*—snatching off the top with the leaves and seeds and was off again before the *Dagûl`kû* knew what had happened.

Before he got home with the tobacco the old woman fainted. They thought she was dead. Hummingbird blew smoke into her nostrils. With the cry, *"Tsâ'lû! Tobacco!"* She opened her eyes and was alive again.

The Hunter and the Hawk

Hunter saw Hawk, *Tlä'nuwa*, overhead. He tried to hide, but the great bird saw him. Sweeping down it struck its claws into the hunter's pack and carried him far up into the air.

As it flew, Hawk told the hunter to not fear. She would not hurt him. She only wanted him to stay for a while with her young ones to guard them until they were old enough to leave the nest.

At last, they arrived at the mouth of a cave in the face of a steep cliff. Inside water dripped from the roof. At the farther end two young birds lived in a nest of sticks.

Hawk set the hunter down and flew away, returning with fresh-killed deer, which it tore in pieces, giving the first piece to the hunter, then feeding the two young hawks.

The hunter stayed in the cave many days until the young birds were nearly grown.

Every day the Hawk would fly away from the nest, returning in the evening with a deer or a bear, of which she always gave the first piece to the hunter.

The hunter grew anxious to see his home again, but Hawk told him not to be uneasy, to wait a little while longer.

At last, he made up his mind to escape from the cave. The next morning, after Hawk had gone, he dragged one of the young birds to the mouth of the cave and tied himself to one of its legs with a strap from his hunting pack. Then with the flat side of his tomahawk, he struck it several times on the head until it was dazed and helpless, and pushed the bird and himself together off the shelf of rock into the air. They fell far down toward the earth, but the air from below held up the bird's wings, so it was almost as if they were flying.

As the baby *Tlä'nuwä* revived it tried to fly upward toward the nest, but the hunter struck it again with his hatchet until it was dazed and dropped again.

At last, they came down in the top of a poplar tree, when the hunter untied the strap from the leg of the young bird letting it fly away, first pulling a feather from its wing.

He climbed down from the tree and went to his home in the settlement, but when he looked in his pack for the feather, he found a stone instead.

It is also known that hawks have little regard except for the great mythic hawk, *Tlää'nuwää'*.

Eagle

Awââ'hiïlïï, is the sacred bird of the Real People.

It is prominent in ceremonial ritual especially in things relating to war. The particular species prized was the golden eagle called by the Real People the "pretty-feathered eagle," because of its beautiful tail feathers.

The killing of an eagle concerns the whole settlement. Only a professional eagle killer chosen for knowledge of prescribed forms and prayers to obtain pardon for the necessary sacrilege and ward off vengeance from the tribe could do it.

When a man deliberately kills an eagle in defiance of the ordinances, he is haunted by dreams of fierce eagles swooping down upon him until the nightmare is exorcised by priestly treatment.

Eagle must be killed only in winter or late fall after crops are gathered and snakes retire to their dens. If killed in summer frost destroys the corn and the songs of the Eagle dance, when the feathers are brought home, angers the snakes so they become doubly dangerous. Consequently, Eagle songs are never sung until after the snakes are asleep for the winter.

When the Real People decide upon an Eagle dance, the eagle killer is called to procure feathers for the occasion. He is paid for his services from offerings at the dance. These professionals guard their secrets carefully from outsiders and their business is a profitable one.

After preliminary preparation, the eagle killer goes alone to the mountains where he prays and fasts after which he kills a deer, placing the body in an exposed site on high cliffs, then conceals himself, singing in a low undertone songs to call down eagles from the sky.

When the eagle alights upon the carcass the hunter shoots it, offers a prayer begging the eagle to not seek vengeance on his tribe, blaming a Spaniard for the deed.

The selection of such a vicarious victim of revenge is evidence of the antiquity of the prayer and of an enduring impression, the cruelties of the early Spaniards made upon the Real People.

The prayer ended, the eagle killer leaves the dead eagle where it fell and hurries to the settlement, where the people anxiously await his return.

On meeting the first warriors he says, "A snowbird has died." And goes at once to his own home, his work finished.

The snowbird announcement insures against the vengeance of any eagles that might overhear. The little snowbird being considered too insignificant a creature to be dreaded.

After four days, insect parasites leave the body and delegated hunters bring in the feathers. They strip the body of the large tail and wing feathers, wrap them in a fresh deerskin and return to the settlement, leaving the body of the dead eagle upon the ground together with that of the slain deer, the latter intended as a sacrifice to the eagle spirits.

In the settlement, the feathers, wrapped in the deerskin, are hung up in a small, round hut built for this special purpose near the edge of the dance ground known as the place "where the feathers are kept," or feather house.

The Eagle dance is held on the night of the same day on which the feathers are brought in with necessary arrangements made beforehand.

To feed the hungry feathers, a dish of venison and corn is set on the ground below them and they are invited to eat. The body of a flaxbird or scarlet tanager is hung up with feathers for the same purpose. The food given to the feathers is disposed of after the dance.

It is also said Eagle is the greatest of warriors and only those versed in the sacred ordinances dare wear the feathers or to carry them in the dance.

Any person who dreams of eagles or eagle feathers must arrange for an Eagle dance, with the usual vigil and fasting, at the first opportunity; otherwise, some one of his family will die.

And should insect parasites, which infest the feathers of the bird in life, get upon a man they will breed a skin disease even though it may be latent for years. It is for this reason the body of the eagle is allowed to remain four days upon the ground before being brought into the settlement.

Owl

There are three owls.

tskïlï', dusky horned owl;
u'guku', barred or hooting owl;
wa`huhu', screech owl.

The first of names signifies a witch, the others onomatopes.

Owls and other night-crying birds are believed to be embodied ghosts or disguised witches, and their cry is dreaded as a sound of evil omen.

If the eyes of a child are bathed with water in which one of the long wing or tail feathers of an owl have been soaked, the child will be able to keep awake all night.

The feather must be found by chance, not procured.

Buzzard the Physician

It is said Buzzard, *Suliï'* is a doctor among birds respected accordingly.

Its feathers are never worn by ball players for fear of becoming bald. Since it thrives on carrion and decay it is believed to be immune from sickness, of a contagious character.

A small quantity of its flesh eaten, or soup used as a wash, is believed to be a sure preventive of smallpox. It was used during the smallpox epidemic among Eastern Cherokee in 1866.

It is said that a buzzard feather placed over a cabin door keeps out witches.

In treating gunshot wounds, the medicine is blown into the wound through a tube cut from a buzzard quill and Buzzard's down is laid over the spot.

Hummingbird and Crane in Love

Hummingbird and Crane loved the same pretty woman.

She preferred Hummingbird, who was handsome.

Crane was awkward, unattractive, and persistent.

To rid her of him, she told him he must challenge Hummingbird to a race and she would marry the winner.

Hummingbird was swift, like a flash of lightning.

Crane slow and heavy.

The pretty woman knew Hummingbird would win. What she did not know was that Crane could fly all night.

They started from her house, flying around the world to the beginning.

From the start Hummingbird darted off, an arrow of color, in and out of sight, moment by moment, his rival far behind.

He flew all day. When evening came, he stopped to roost for the night. He was far ahead.

Crane flew steadily all night long, passed Hummingbird in the night, going until he came to a creek, stopped and rested at daylight.

Hummingbird awakened in the morning, flying and thinking how easily he would win the race, until he reached the creek. There he found Crane spearing breakfast tadpoles with his long bill.

Surprised, Hummingbird wondered at this. How could it happen? He flew swiftly by leaving Crane out of sight again.

Crane finished his breakfast and started again. When evening came, he kept on as before. It was hardly midnight when he passed Hummingbird asleep on a limb.

In the morning, he finished breakfast as Hummingbird caught up again. The next day he gained a little more.

On the fourth day, he was spearing tadpoles for dinner when Hummingbird passed him. On the fifth and sixth days, it was late in the afternoon when Hummingbird caught up.

On the seventh day, Crane was a whole night's travel ahead. He took his time at breakfast, fixed himself up as nicely as he could at the creek, coming in early in the morning at the starting place where the woman lived.

When Hummingbird arrived in the afternoon, he found he had lost the race, but the woman declared she would never have such an ugly fellow as Crane for a husband, so she remained single for all time.

Mudhen

Mudhen is called *diga'gwanïï'*, lame or crippled, because it flies only a short distance at a time.

In the *Diga'gwanïï* dance performers sing the name of the bird endeavoring to imitate its halting movements.

Turkey's Neck

After Terrapin won the race from Rabbit, other animals wondered about it because Terrapin was so slow. However, they also knew he was a warrior with conjuring secrets.

Turkey was not satisfied. He told the others there must be some trick about it.

He said, "I know the Terrapin can't run. He can hardly crawl. I'm going to try him."

One day Turkey met Terrapin coming home from war with a fresh scalp hanging from his neck dragging on the ground as he traveled.

Turkey laughed at the sight saying, "That scalp don't look right on you. Your neck is too short and low down to wear it that way. Let me show you."

Terrapin agreed. He gave the scalp to Turkey, who fastened it around his neck.

Turkey said, "Now, I'll walk a little way. You can see how it looks."

He walked ahead a short distance, turned asking Terrapin how he liked it.

Terrapin said, "It looks very nice. It becomes you."

Turkey said, "Now I'll fix it a different way and let you see how it looks."

He gave the string another pull, walking ahead.

Terrapin said, "O, that looks very nice."

Turkey kept walking. When Terrapin called to him to bring back the scalp, he walked faster breaking into a run. Terrapin got his bow shooting cane splints into Turkey's leg to cripple him so that he could not run. Therefore, all small bones in the Turkey's leg are of no use.

Terrapin never caught Turkey, who still wears the scalp around his neck like a beard.

How Turkey Got His Gobble

All animals and birds used to play ball in the old days. They were proud of cheers just as ball players today are proud of cheers. Grouse had a fine voice he used in ball play. Turkey did not have a good voice. So, he asked Grouse to give him lessons.

Grouse agreed to teach him for a price. Turkey promised to give him some feathers to make himself a collar.

That is how Grouse got his collar of turkey feathers.

They began lessons and Turkey learned very fast. Finally, Grouse thought it was time to try Turkey's voice.

Grouse said, "Now, I'll stand on this hollow log and when I give the signal by tapping on it, you cheer as loudly as you can."

He got upon a hollow log ready to tap on it, as a Grouse still does. When he gave the signal Turkey was so eager and excited he could not raise his voice for a cheer. He gobbled.

Ever since he gobbles whenever he hears a noise.

Bird Calls

Many bird names reflect their call.

Wa`huhu' screech owl,

U'guku' hooting owl,

Kââgûû crow,

Güügwëë' quail,

Huhu yellow mocking-bird,

Tsïï'küülïï' chickadee,

S*a'sa'* goose,

Gulëë'-diska`nihïï' turtledove, crying for acorns reflecting the word for acorn -- *gulëë'*.

Nääkwïïsïï' meadowlark because its tail when spread out in flight looks like a star.

Sitta carolinensis nuthatch is said to be deaf, because it seems to be fearless in human presence.

The Great Mythic Hawk

On the north bank of Little Tennessee River, in a bend below the mouth of Citico Creek, in Blount County, Tennessee, a high cliff hangs over the water. Half way up the face of the rock is a cave with two openings. The rock projects outward above the cave, so the mouth cannot be seen from above. It seems impossible to reach the cave from above or below. There are white streaks in the rock from the cave down to the water.

The Real People call it *Tlä'nuwâ'ï*, "the place of the great mythic hawk."

In the old time, soon after the creation, a pair of *Tlä'nuwäs* had their nest in this cave. Their droppings made streaks in the rock. They were immense birds, larger than any that live now, strong and savage. They were forever flying up and down the river coming to the settlements to carry off dogs and young children playing near the houses.

No one could reach the nest to kill them and when the Real People tried to shoot them the arrows glanced off, were seized and carried away in the talons of the *Tlä'nuwäs*.

At last, the Real People went to a great medicine man who promised to help them. Some were afraid that if he failed to kill the *Tlä'nuwäs* they would take revenge on the people, but the medicine man said he could fix that.

He made a long rope of bark, just as the Real People still do, with loops in it for his feet. He had the People let him down from the top of the cliff when he knew the old birds were away.

Once opposite the month of the cave but he still could not reach it because the rock above hung over. Therefore, he swung himself back and forth several times until the rope swung near enough for him to pull himself into the cave with a hooked stick that he carried.

In the nest, he found four young ones. On the floor

of the cave were the bones of all sorts of animals that had been carried there by the hawks. He pulled the young ones out of the nest, throwing them over the cliff into the deep water below where a great *Uktena* serpent lived, who finished them.

Just then, he saw the two old ones coming and barely had time to climb up again to the top of the rock before they reached the nest. When they found the nest empty they were furious.

They circled round and round in the air until they saw the snake put up its head from the water. Then they darted down and one seized the snake in his talons and flew far up in the sky with it, his mate struck at it, bit off piece after piece until nothing was left. They were so high up that when the pieces fell they made holes in the rock, which are still to be seen there at the place the Real People call "Where the *Tlä'nuwä* cut it up."

Then the two *Tlä'nuwäs* circled up until they went out of sight. They have never been seen since.

Why Owl is Skinny

A widow with one daughter warned the girl that she must get a good hunter for a husband when she married. The young woman listened and promised to do as her mother advised.

At last, a suitor came to ask the mother for the girl, but the widow told him that only a good hunter could have her daughter.

Said the lover, "I'm just that kind."

He again asked her to speak for him to the young woman. Therefore, the mother went to the girl and told her a young man had come courting and as he said, he was a good hunter she advised her daughter to take him.

The girl said, "Just as you say."

Therefore, when he came again, the matter was all arranged and he went to live with the girl. The next morning he got ready and said he would go out hunting. Before starting, he changed his mind and said he would go fishing. He was gone all day and came home late at night, bringing only three small fish, saying that he had no luck, but would have better success to-morrow.

The next morning he started again to fish and was gone all day, but came home at night with only two small spring lizards and the same excuse. The next day he said he would go hunting this time. He was gone again until night and returned at last with only a handful of scraps he had found where some hunters had cut up a deer.

By this time, the old woman was suspicious. So next morning when he started out again to fish, she told her daughter to follow him secretly and see how he set to work. The girl followed through the woods and kept him in sight until he came down to the river. She saw her husband change to Hooting Owl (*uguku'*) and fly over to a pile of driftwood in the water and cry, "*U-gu-ku! hu! hu! u! u!*"

She was surprised and very angry.

She said to herself, "I thought I had married a man, but my husband is only an owl."

She watched and saw the owl look into the water for a long time and at last swoop down and bring up in his claws a handful of sand from which he picked out a crawfish. Then he flew across to the bank, took the form of a man again and started home with the crawfish.

His wife hurried ahead through the woods. When he came in with the crawfish in his hand, she asked him where all the fish he had caught were. He said he had none, because an owl had frightened them all away.

"I think you are the owl," said his wife and drove him out of the house.

The owl went into the woods and there he pined away with grief and love until there was no flesh left on any part of his body except his head.

Why Buzzard's Head is Bare

Buzzard once had a fine topknot of which he was so proud he refused to eat carrion and while other birds pecked at the body of a deer or other animal, he would strut and say, "You may have it all, it is not good enough for me."

Because of his excessive pride, Buzzard lost not only his topknot but nearly all the other feathers on his head. And now, he must eat carrion for a living.

How Kingfisher Got His Bill

Kingfisher was meant to be a water bird but was not given web feet or a good bill, so he could not make a living.

The animals held a council, deciding to make him a bill like a long sharp awl for a fishgig, fastening it front of his mouth.

He flew to the top of a tree, sailed out, darted down into water, came up with a fish on his gig. And he has been the best gigger ever since.

It is said by others that Kingfisher got his bill another way.

They say Blacksnake found Yellowhammer's nest in a hollow tree and after swallowing the young birds, coiled up to sleep in the nest where the mother bird found him when she came home. She went for help to the Little People, who sent her to the Kingfisher.

He came and after flew back and forth past the hole a few times, made one dart at the snake pulling him out dead.

When they looked they found a hole in the snake's head where Kingfisher pierced it with a slender *tugälû'nä* fish, he carried in his bill like a lance.

From this, the Little People concluded he would make a first-class gigger if he only had the right spear, so they gave him his long bill as a reward.

How Partridge Got His Whistle

Terrapin had a fine whistle.

Partridge had none.

Terrapin was constantly whistling until Partridge became jealous.

One day Partridge asked to try Terrapin's whistle.

Terrapin was afraid to risk it at first.

However, Partridge said, "I'll give it back right away. If you are afraid you can stay with me while I practice."

Terrapin let him have the whistle. Partridge walked around blowing on it in fine fashion.

Partridge asked, "How does it sound with me?"

Terrapin answered, "O, you do very well."

Partridge ran ahead whistling faster saying, "Now, how do you like it."

Terrapin answered, "That's fine, but don't run so fast."

Partridge spread his wings, gave a long low whistle and flew to the top of tree, saying, "And now, how do you like this?"

Poor Terrapin looked up from the ground. He never recovered his whistle. From that and the loss of his scalp, Turkey stole from him, he grew ashamed to be seen. Ever since he shuts himself up in his box when anyone comes near him.

How Redbird Got His Color

Raccoon passed Wolf one day and made several insulting remarks, until at last Wolf became angry, turned and chased him. Raccoon ran his best managing to reach a tree by the riverside before Wolf caught up with him.

He climbed the tree and stretched out on a limb overhanging the water. When Wolf arrived, he saw the reflection in the water and thinking it was Raccoon he jumped at it and was nearly drowned before he could scramble out again, all wet and dripping.

He lay down on the bank to dry and fell asleep and while he slept Raccoon came down from the tree and plastered his eves with dung. When Wolf awoke, he found he could not open his eyes, and began to whine. Along came a little brown bird, through the bushes heard Wolf crying, and asked what the matter was.

Wolf told his story and said, "If you will get my eves open, I will show you where to find some nice red paint to paint yourself."

The little brown bird said, "All right."

Then he pecked at Wolf's eyes until he got off all the plaster. Wolf took him to a rock that had streaks of bright red paint running through it and the little bird painted himself with it and has ever since been a Redbird.

Eagle's Revenge

Once a hunter in the mountains heard a noise at night like a rushing wind outside his cabin and going out he found an eagle had alighted on the drying pole and was tearing at the body of a deer hanging there. Without thinking of the danger, he shot the eagle.

In the morning, he took the deer and started back to the settlement, where he told what he had done. The chief sent some men to bring in the eagle and arrange for an Eagle dance. They brought back the dead eagle. Everything was made ready and that night they started the dance in the townhouse.

About midnight there was a whoop outside and a strange warrior came into the circle and began to recite his exploits. No one knew him, but they thought he had come from one of the farther towns of the Real People. He told how he had killed a man, and at the end of the story, he gave a hoarse yell, "Hi!"

It startled the whole company and one of the seven men with the rattles fell over dead. He sang of another deed and at the end straightened up with another loud yell. A second rattler fell dead and the people were so full of fear that they could not stir from their places. Still he kept on, and at every pause, there came again that terrible scream until the last of the seven rattlers fell dead. Then the stranger went out into the darkness. Long afterward, they learned from the eagle killer that it was the brother of the eagle shot by the hunter.

Immortals, Spirits and Monsters

The People Who Live Anywhere

Immortals, *Nûûññëë'hïï* the "people who live anywhere," were a race of spirit people living in the highlands of the old Cherokee country.

They had a many townhouses, especially in the bald mountains, the high peaks above timberline on timber ever grows. They had large townhouses at Pilot Knob, under the old *Nïïkwääsïï'* mound in North Carolina and under Blood Mountain at the head of Nottely River in Georgia.

They were invisible except when they wanted to be seen and then they looked and spoke like other Indians. They were very fond of music and dancing and hunters in the mountains would often hear the dance, the songs, the drum beating in some invisible townhouse.

However, when they went toward the sound it would shift about and they would hear it behind them or away in some other direction, so they could never find the place where the dance was.

They were a friendly people often bringing lost wanderers to their townhouses under the mountains caring for them until they rested and then guided them back to their home.

More than once, when the Real People were hard pressed by an enemy, the *Nûûññëë'hïï* warriors came to save them from defeat.

Some people think they are the same as the *Yûûññwïï Tsunsdi'*, the "Little People"; but these are fairies, no larger in size than children.

The Boy and the Immortals

There was a man in Nottely town who had been with the *Nûûññnëë'hïï* when he was a boy.

He was a truthful, but hardheaded and his story began when he was about ten or twelve years old.

Playing one day near the river, he shot at a mark with his bow and arrows. He became tired and started to build a fish trap in the water. While he was piling up stones in two long walls, a man came and stood on the bank asking him what he was doing.

The boy told him and the man said, "Well, that's pretty hard work. You ought to rest a while. Come and take a walk up the river."

The boy said, "No."

He was going home to dinner soon.

The stranger said, "Come to my house. I'll give you a good dinner and bring you home again in the morning."

The boy went with him up the river until they came to a house and when they went in the man's wife and other people there were very glad to see him. They gave him a fine dinner and were very kind to him.

While they were eating, a man the boy knew well came in and spoke to him, so he felt quite at home. After dinner, he played with the other children and slept there that night.

After breakfast, the next morning the man took him home. They went down a path with a cornfield on one side, a peach orchard on the other until they came to another trail.

The man said, "Go along this trail across that ridge and you will come to the river road that will bring you straight to your home."

Then, the man went back to his house and the boy went on along the trail. When he had gone a little way he looked back. There was no cornfield or orchard or fence or house; nothing but trees on the mountainside.

He thought it odd, but he was not frightened and continued on until he came to the river trail in sight of his home. Many people were standing talking and when they saw him, they ran toward him shouting,

"Here he is! He is not drowned or killed in the mountains!"

They had been hunting him ever since yesterday noon. They asked him where he had been.

The boy said, "A man took me to his house just across the ridge. I had a fine dinner and a good time with the children. I thought *Udsi'skalää* here, the name of the man he had seen at dinner, would tell you where I was."

Udsi'skalää said, "I haven't seen you. I was out all day in my canoe hunting you. It was one of the *Nûûññnëë'hïï* that made himself look like me."

The boy's mother said, "You say you had dinner there?"

The boy answered, "Yes, and I had plenty, too."

His mother replied, "There is no house there. Only trees and rocks. But sometimes we hear a drum in the big bald above. The people you saw were *Nûûññnëë'hïï.*"

Water Cannibals

A race of cannibal spirits lives at the bottom of deep rivers living on human flesh, especially that of little children.

They come out just after daybreak, going about unseen from house to house until they find some one asleep. Then, they shoot him with invisible arrows; carry the dead body down under the water to feast upon it.

That no one may know what has happened they leave in place of the body an image of the dead man or little child.

The image wakes up talks and goes about just as he always did, but there is no life in it. In seven days, it withers and dies. The people bury it and think they are burying their dead friend.

It was a long time before the Real People found out about this. Now, they always try to be awake at daylight and wake up the children, telling them, "The hunters are among you."

The Prosperous Trader

Long before the white man's revolution, *Yahula* was a prosperous trader among the Real People. The tinkling of bells hung around the necks of his ponies could be heard on every mountain trail.

Once there was a great hunt and all the warriors were out. When it was over and they were ready to return to the settlement, *Yahula* was not with them. They waited and searched, but he could not be found. At last, they went back without him and his friends grieved for him as for one dead.

Some time after, his people were surprised and delighted to have him walk in among them and sit down while they were at supper.

He told them he had been lost in the mountains and the *Nûñnë'hï*, the Immortals, found him and brought him to their town where he had been kept ever since.

They gave him only the kindest care and treatment until the longing to see his old friends brought him back.

When his friends invited him to eat with them, he said that it was now too late. He had tasted fairy food and never again could he eat with human kind. For the same reason he could not stay with his family. He had to go back to the *Nûñnë'hï*.

His wife, children and brother begged him to stay, but he could not. It was either life with the Immortals or death with his own people. After further discussion he rose to go.

They saw him as he sat talking to them and as he stood up, but the moment he stepped out door he vanished.

He came back often to visit his people. They would see him first, as he entered the house, and while he sat and talked he was his old self in every way, but the instant he stepped across the threshold he was gone, though a hundred eyes might be watching.

He came often, but at last their entreaties grew so urgent that the *Nûññë'hï* must have been offended. He came no more.

***

On the mountain at the head of Yahoola Creek, some ten miles above Dahlonega, is a small square enclosure of uncut stone, without roof or entrance. Here it was said he lived. The Real People call it *Yahulâ's* and call the stream by the same name.

Often at night, a late traveler coming along the trail by the creek hears the voice of *Yahula* singing certain favorite old songs he used to like to sing as he drove his pack of horses across the mountain. The sound of his voice urges them on. The crack of a whip and the tinkling of bells go with the song. However, neither driver nor horses are seen. And the songs and the bells are heard only at night.

One man who was Yahulâ's friend sang the same songs for a time after he had disappeared, but he died suddenly. The Real People are afraid to sing these songs any more.

When the Real People went to Indian Territory in 1838 some of them said, "Maybe Yahula has gone there and we shall hear him,"

However, they never heard him again.

Immortal Women Come to Dance

Four *Nûûññnëë'hïï* women came to a dance at the settlement. They danced half the night with the young men. No one knew they were *Nûûññnëë'hïï*. They thought them visitors from another settlement. Then, about midnight they left to go home.

Some men who had come out from the townhouse to cool off watched to see which way they went. The women went down the trail to the river ford and just as they came to the water, they disappeared, although it was a plain trail with no place where they could hide. Then the watchers knew they were *Nûûññnëë'hïï* women. Several men saw this happen.

One of them was known as an honest man who always told the truth.

Immortal Voices

In ancient times, the Real People heard the voices of invisible spirits calling and warning them of wars and misfortunes, which the future held.

The voices invited them to come and live with the *Nûûññëë'hïï*, the Immortals, in their homes under the mountains and waters. For many days, the voices hung in the air.

The spirits said, "If you will live with us gather everyone in your townhouses, fast for seven days and let no one must raise a shout or a war whoop in all that time. Do this and we shall come and you will see us and we shall take you to live with us."

The Real People were afraid. They knew the Immortals of the mountains and waters were happy forever, so they counseled in their townhouses and decided to go with them.

They gathered in their townhouse, prayed and fasted for six days. On the seventh day, there was a sound from the distant mountains. It came nearer and grew louder until Thunder's roar was heard all about the townhouse. They felt the ground shake under them. They were frightened and despite the warning, some of them screamed.

The *Nûûññëë'hïï*, who had already lifted the townhouse with its mound to carry it away were startled by the cry and dropped it where we see it today as the mound of *Sëë`tsïï*.

Then they steadied themselves bearing the rest to the top of *Tsuda'ye`lûûññ'yïï*, Lone Peak, near the head of Cheowa River, where it is still seen, changed long ago to solid rock. The people who live there are invisible and immortal.

The Real People along Shooting Creek prayed and fasted. At the end of seven days the *Nûûññëë'hïï* came, taking them under the water.

They are there now.

***

On a warm summer day when the wind ripples the surface, those who listen well can hear them talking below.

When the Real People drag the river for fish, the fish-drag always catches there although the water is deep.

The Real People know it is being held by their lost kinsmen who do not want to be forgotten.

When the Real People were removed to the West one of the greatest regrets was they were compelled to leave behind relatives who had gone to the *Nûûññëë'hïï*.

Fish and Frogs

It is said fish and frogs came from one monster doing much damage until killed by the Real People, who cut it in little pieces, threw it into water, to take the shape of small fish and frogs.

Bear Man

A man went hunting in the mountains and came across a black bear, which he wounded with an arrow. The bear turned and started to run the other way, and the hunter followed, shooting one arrow after another into it without bringing it down. Now, this was Medicine Bear, who could talk or read the thoughts of people without their saying a word.

At last, he stopped, pulled the arrows out of his side and gave them to the man, saying, "It is of no use for you to shoot at me, for you can not kill me. Come to my house and let us live together."

The hunter thought to himself, "He may kill me."

Medicine Bear read his thoughts and said, "No, I won't hurt you."

The man thought again, "How can I get anything to eat?"

Medicine Bear knew his thoughts, and said, "There shall be plenty."

Therefore, the hunter went with Medicine Bear. They traveled together until they came to a hole in the side of the mountain.

Medicine Bear said, "This is not where I live, but there is going to be a council here and we will see what they do."

They went in, and the hole widened as they entered until they came to a large cave like a townhouse. It was full of bears--old bears, young bears, and cubs, white bears, black bears, and brown bears--and a large white bear was the chief. They sat down in a corner, but soon the bears scented the hunter.

They asked, "What is it that smells bad?"

The chief said, "Don't talk so. It is only a stranger come to see us. Let him alone."

Food was getting scarce in the mountains and the council was to decide what to do about it. They sent out messengers and while they were talking two bears came in and reported that they had found a country in the low grounds where there, were so many chestnuts and acorns that mast was knee deep.

They were all pleased, and got ready for a dance, and the dance leader was called *Kalâs'-gûnähi'ta,* "Long Hams," a great black bear that is always lean. After the dance, the bears noticed the hunter's bow and arrows.

One said, "This is what men use to kill us. Let us see if we can manage them, and maybe we can fight man with his own weapons."

So they took the bow and arrows from the hunter to try them. They fitted the arrow and drew back the string, but when they let go it caught in their long claws and the arrows dropped to the ground. They saw that they could not use the bow and arrows and gave them back to the man. When the dance and the council were over, they all began to go home, excepting the White Bear chief, who lived there. The hunter and Medicine Bear went on until they came to another hole in the side of the mountain.

Medicine Bear said, "This is where I live."

They went in. By this time, the hunter was very hungry. He wondered how he could get something to eat. Medicine Bear knew his thoughts and sitting up on his hind legs he rubbed his stomach with his forepaws and at once he had both paws full of chestnuts and gave them to the man. He rubbed his stomach again, had his paws full of huckleberries, and gave them to the man. He rubbed again and gave the man both paws full of blackberries. He rubbed again and had his paws full of acorns, but the man said that he could not eat them, and that he had enough already.

The hunter lived in the cave with Medicine Bear all winter, until long hair like that of a bear began to grow all over his body and he began to act like a bear. However, he still walked like a man.

In early spring Medicine Bear said to him, "Your

people down in the settlement are getting ready for a grand hunt in these mountains, and they will come to this cave and kill me and take these clothes from me"—he meant his skin—"but they will not hurt you and will take you home with them."

Medicine Bear knew what the people were doing down in the settlement. He always knew what the man was thinking.

Some days passed and Medicine Bear said again, "This is the day when the Topknots will come to kill me, but the Split-noses will come first and find us. When they have killed me, they will drag me outside the cave, take off my clothes, and cut me in pieces. You must cover the blood with leaves and when they are taking you away look back after you have gone a piece and you will see something."

Soon they heard hunters coming up the mountain and then the dogs found the cave and began to bark. The hunters came and looked inside and saw Medicine Bear and killed him with their arrows. Then they dragged him outside the cave, skinned the body, and cut it in quarters to carry home. The dogs kept on barking until the hunters thought there must be another bear in the cave. They looked in again and saw the man away at the farther end.

At first, they thought it was another bear because of his long hair, but it was the hunter who had been lost the year before. They went in and brought him out. Then each hunter took a load of the bear meat and they started home bringing the man and the skin with them. Before they left, the man piled leaves over the spot where they had cut up the bear and when they had gone he looked behind and saw Medicine Bear rise up out of the leaves, shake himself, and go back into the woods.

When they came near the settlement, the man told the hunters that he must be shut up where no one could see him without anything to eat or drink for seven days and nights, until the bear nature had left him and he became like a man again. Therefore, they shut him up alone in a house and tried to keep very still about it. However, the news got out and his wife heard of it. She came for her husband, but the people would not let her near him. Still, she came every day and begged so hard that after four or five days they let her have him.

She took him home with her, but in a short time, he died because he still had a bear's nature and could not live like a man. If they had kept him shut up and fasting until the end of the seven days he would have become a man again and would have lived.

Spear Finger

Long, long ago there dwelt in the mountains a terrible ogre, a woman monster, whose food was human livers.

She could take any shape or appearance to suit her purpose. In her right form, she looked like an old woman, except that her whole body was covered with a skin as hard as a rock that no weapon could wound or penetrate. On her right hand she had a long, stony forefinger of bone like an awl or spearhead with which she stabbed everyone to whom she could get near enough.

Because of this she was called U`tlûñ'tä "Spear-Finger." Because of her stony skin she was sometimes called Nûñ'yunu'ï, "Stone-Dress."

Spear-finger had such powers over stone that she could easily lift and carry immense rocks and could cement them together by merely striking one against another. To get over rough country more easily she built a great rock bridge through the air from Nûñyû'-tlu`gûñ'yï, the "Tree Rock," on Hiwassee River, over to Sanigilâ'gï (Whiteside Mountain) on the Blue Ridge. It started from the top of the "Tree Rock" when lightning struck it and scattered the fragments along the whole ridge where those who go there can still see the pieces.

She used to range all over the mountains about the heads of the streams and in the dark passes of *Nantahala*, always hungry and looking for victims. Her favorite haunt on the Tennessee side was about the gap on the trail where Chilhowee Mountain comes down to the river.

Sometimes an old woman would approach along the trail where the children were picking strawberries or playing near the village.

She would say to them coaxingly, "Come, my grandchildren, come to your granny and let granny dress your hair."

When some little girl ran up, laid her head in the old woman's lap to be petted and combed the old witch would gently run her fingers through the child's hair until it went to sleep. Then she would stab the little one through the heart or back of the neck with the long awl finger, which she had kept hidden under her robe. Then she would take out the liver and eat it.

She would enter a house by taking the appearance of one of the family who happened to have gone out for a short time and would watch her chance to stab someone with her long finger and take out his liver. She could stab him without being noticed and often the victim did not even know it at the time because it left no wound and caused no pain. The victim went about his affairs until all at once he felt weak and gradually to pined away and died because Spear-Finger had taken his liver.

When the Real People went out in the fall to burn leaves off the mountains to get the chestnuts on the ground, they were never safe. The old witch was always on the lookout. As soon as she saw the smoke rise she knew there were Indians there and sneaked up to try to surprise one alone. So they tried to keep together and were cautious of allowing any stranger to approach the camp. However, if one went down to the spring for a drink, they never knew when the liver eater would come and sit with them.

Sometimes she took her proper form, and once or twice, when far out from the settlements, a solitary hunter saw an old woman, with a queer-looking hand, going through the woods singing low to herself, "*Uwe'la na'tsïkû'. Su' sä' sai'*. Liver, I eat it. *Su' sa' sai'*.

It was rather a pretty song, but it chilled his blood for he knew it was the liver eater and he hurried away, silently, before she might see him.

At last a great council was held to devise some means to get rid of *U`tlûñ'tä* before she should destroy everybody. The people came from all around, and after much talk, they decided that the best way would be to trap her in a pitfall where all the warriors could attack her at once.

Therefore, they dug a deep pitfall across the trail and covered it over with earth and grass as if the ground had never been disturbed. Then they kindled a large fire of brush near the trail and hid themselves in the laurels, because they knew she would come as soon as she saw the smoke.

Sure enough, they soon saw an old woman coming along the trail. She looked like an old woman whom they knew well in the village and although several of the wiser men wanted to shoot at her, the others interfered. They did not want to hurt one of their own people.

The old woman came slowly along the trail with one hand under her blanket. She stepped upon the pitfall and tumbled through the brush top into the deep hole below. At once, she showed her true nature and instead of the feeble old woman there was the terrible U'tlûñ'tä with her stony skin, her sharp awl finger reaching out in every direction for some one to stab.

The hunters rushed out from the thicket and surrounded the pit. They shot as true and as often as they could, but their arrows struck the stony mail of the witch only to be broken and fall useless at her feet. She taunted them and tried to climb out of the pit to get at them.

They kept out of her way, but were only wasting their arrows when a small bird, Utsu''gï, the titmouse, perched on a tree overhead and began to sing, "*un, un, un.*"

They thought it was saying *u'nahü'*, heart, meaning that they should aim at the heart of the stone witch. They directed their arrows where the heart should be, but the arrows only glanced off with the flintheads broken. Then they caught the Utsu''gï and cut off its tongue, so that ever since its tongue is short and everybody knows it is a liar. When the hunters let it go it flew straight up into the sky until it was out of sight and never came back again. The titmouse that we know now is only an image of the other.

They kept up the fight without result until another bird, little *Tsï'kïlilï'*, the chickadee, flew down from a tree and alighted upon the witch's right hand. The warriors took this as a sign that they must aim there. They were right, for her heart was on the inside of her hand which she kept doubled into a fist, the same awl hand with which she had stabbed so many people.

Now she was frightened in earnest and began to rush furiously at them with her long awl finger and to jump about in the pit to dodge the arrows. At last a lucky arrow struck just where the awl joined her wrist and she fell down dead.

Ever since the *tsï'kïlilï'* is known as a truth teller. When a man is away on a journey and this bird comes and perches near the house and chirps its song, his friends know he will soon be safe home.

Stone Man

Once when all the people of the settlement were out in the mountains on a great hunt one man who had gone on ahead climbed to the top of a high ridge and found a large river on the other side.

While he was looking across, he saw an old man walking on the opposite ridge with a cane that seemed to be made of some bright, shining rock. The hunter watched and saw that every little while the old man would point his cane in a certain direction, then draw it back and smell the end of it. At last, he pointed it in the direction of the hunting camp on the other side of the mountain and this time when he drew back the staff he sniffed it several times as if it smelled very good. He then started along the ridge straight for the camp.

With the help of the cane, he moved very slowly until he reached the end of the ridge. Then he threw the cane out into the air and it became a bridge of shining rock stretching across the river. After he had crossed over on the bridge, it became a cane again and the old man picked it up and started over the mountain toward the camp.

The hunter was frightened and felt sure it meant mischief, so he hurried on down the mountain and took the shortest trail back to the camp to get there before the old man. When he got there and told his story the medicine-man said the old man was a wicked cannibal monster called *Nûñ'yunu'wï*, "Dressed in Stone."

He lived in that part of the country, and was always going about the mountains looking for some hunter to kill and eat. It was very hard to escape from him because his stick guided him like a dog. It was nearly as hard to kill him, because his whole body was covered with a skin of solid rock.

If he came, he would kill and eat them all. There was only one way to save them. He could not bear to look upon a menstrual woman. If they could find seven menstrual women to stand in the path as he came along the sight would kill him.

Therefore, they asked among all the women and found seven who were menstruating. With one of them, it had just begun. By the order of the medicine man, they stripped themselves and stood along the path where the old man would come. Soon they heard *Nûñ'yunu'wï* coming through the woods, feeling his way with his stone cane.

He came along the trail to where the first woman was standing, and as soon as he saw her, he started and cried out,

"*Yu!* My grandchild; you are in a very bad state!"

He hurried past her, but in a moment he met the next woman, and cried out again, "*Yu!* My child; you are in a terrible way."

He again hurried past her only now he was vomiting blood. He hurried on and met the third, the fourth, and the fifth woman. With each one his step grew weaker until when he came to the last one, with whom the sickness had just begun. The blood poured from his mouth and he fell down on the trail. Then the medicine man drove seven sourwood stakes through his body and pinned him to the ground. When night came, they piled great logs over him and set fire to them and all the people gathered around to see.

Nûñ'yunu'wï was a great *ada'wehï* and knew many secrets. As the fire came close to him, he began to talk and told them the medicine for all kinds of sickness. At midnight he began to sing. He sang hunting songs for calling up the bear and the deer and all the animals of the woods and mountains. As the blaze grew hotter, his voice sank lower and lower until at last when daylight came and the logs were a heap of white ashes and the voice was still.

Then the medicine man told them to rake off the ashes. Where the body had lain they found only a large lump of red *wâ'dï* paint and a magic *u'lûñsû'ti* stone. He kept the stone for himself and calling the people around him he painted them on face and breast with the red *wâ'dï*.

Whatever each person prayed for while the painting was being done-whether for hunting success, for working skill, or for a long life-that gift was his.

Burnt-Tobacco and the Immortals

Crossing a ridge Burnt-Tobacco heard a drum and the songs of dancers in the hills on one side of the trail.

He rode over to see who could be dancing in such a place. When he reached the spot, the drum and the songs were behind him.

He was frightened. He hurried back to the trail riding hard all the way to the settlement to tell the story.

He was a truthful man and they believed what he said.

There must have been many *Nûûññnëë'hïï,* Immortals, in that neighborhood, because drumming was often heard in the high mountains.

Fire under the Mountain

On a small river branch, running nearly due north from Blood Mountain there once was a hole that looked like a small well or chimney from which came a warm vapor heating all the air around.

The Real People said this was because the *Nûûññnëë'hïï* had a townhouse and a fire under the mountain.

Sometimes in cold weather, hunters stop there to warm themselves, but they were afraid to stay long.

Townhouse of the Immortals

Close to the old trading path from South Carolina to the Cherokee Nation, near the head of Tugaloo River, there was a noted waist deep circular depression about the size of a townhouse. Inside it was always clean as though swept by unknown hands.

Passing traders threw logs and rocks into it, but on their return, they would find them thrown far out from the hole.

The Indians said it was a *Nûûññnëë'hïï* townhouse.

They never liked to go near the place or talk about it.

One day some logs thrown in by traders were allowed to remain there and they concluded the *Nûûññnëë'hïï*, annoyed by the persecution of white men, abandoned their townhouse forever.

Where They Cried

Long ago, a powerful tribe invaded the country killing people and destroying settlements. No leader could stand against them. They laid waste to all the lower settlements and advanced into the mountains.

The warriors of the old town at the head of Little Tennessee, gathered wives and children into the townhouse and kept scouts constantly on the lookout for danger.

One morning before daybreak, scouts saw the enemy approaching and gave the alarm. The men, seizing arms rushed to meet the attack. After a long, hard fight, They were overpowered and retreated.

Suddenly a stranger stood among them shouting to the chief to call off his men. He would drive back the enemy.

From the dress and language of the stranger the Real People thought he was a chief who had come with reinforcements from the over hill settlements in Tennessee.

They fell back along the trail and as they came near the townhouse, they saw a great company of warriors coming out of the mound as through an open doorway. Then they knew their friends were *Nûññë'hï*, Immortals, though no one had heard that they lived under the settlement's mound.

The *Nûññë'hï* poured out by the hundreds, armed and painted for the fight. They became invisible as soon as they were outside the settlement, so the enemy saw the arrows, felt the tomahawks, and fell before the onslaught, but could not see who attacked.

Before these invisible foes, the invaders retreated south along the ridge to where it joins the main ridge separating the French Broad from the Tuckasegee River turning with it to the northeast. As they retreated they tried to shield themselves behind rocks and trees, but the *Nûññë'hï* arrows went around the rocks killing them from the other side. They could find no hiding place. All along the ridge they fell, until they reached the head of Tuckasegee. Only half-a-dozen remained alive. In despair they sat down crying for mercy.

Ever since the Real People have called the place *Dayûlsûñ'yï*, "Where they cried."

The *Nûññë'hï* chief told them they deserved their punishment for attacking a peaceful tribe and he spared their lives, telling them to go home and take the news to their people.

This was Indian custom, always spare a few to carry back the news of defeat. They went home and the *Nûññë'hï* went back to the mound.

They are still there.

The Slant-Eyed Giant

A long time ago, a widow lived with her daughter at the old town of *Känuga* on Pigeon River. The girl was of age to marry and her mother used to tell her to make sure to take no one but a good hunter for a husband, so they would have some one to take care of him or her and always have plenty of meat in the house. The girl said such a man was hard to find, but her mother advised her not to be in a hurry and to wait until the right one came.

The mother slept in the house while the girl slept outside in the *âsï*. One dark night a stranger came to the *âsï* wanting to court the girl. She told him her mother would let her marry no one but a good hunter.

The stranger said, "Well, I am a great hunter."

So she let him come in and he stayed all night. Just before day, he said he must go back now to his own place, but that he had brought some meat for her mother and she would find it outside. Then he went away.

When day came, she went out and found a deer. She brought it into the house to her mother and told her it was a present from her new sweetheart. Her mother was pleased and they had deer steaks for breakfast.

He came again the next night, but again went away before daylight. This time he left two deer outside. The mother was more pleased this time.

She said to her daughter, "I wish your sweetheart would bring us some wood."

Now wherever he might be, the stranger knew their thoughts, so when he came the next time he said to the girl, "Tell your mother I have brought the wood."

When she looked out in the morning there were several great trees lying in front of the door, roots and branches and all. The old woman was angry.

She said, "He might have brought us some wood that

we could use instead of whole trees that we can't split, to litter up the road with brush."

The hunter knew what she said and the next time he came, he brought nothing. And when they looked out in the morning the trees were gone and there was no wood at all. So the old woman had to go after some herself.

Almost every night he came to see the girl. Each time he brought a deer or other game. He always left before daylight.

At last, her mother said to her, "Your husband always leaves before daylight. Why don't he wait? I want to see what kind of a son-in-law I have."

When the girl told this to her husband, he said he could not let the old woman see him, because the sight would frighten her.

As she began to the girl said, "She wants to see you, anyhow."

He had to consent, but warned her that her mother must not say that he looked frightful. The next morning he did not leave so early, but stayed in the *âsï*. When it was daylight, the girl went out and told her mother. The old woman came and looked and there she saw a great giant, with long slanting eyes (*tsul`kälû'*), lying doubled up on the floor with his head against the rafters in the left-hand corner at the back. His toes scraped the roof in the right-hand corner by the door.

She gave only one look and ran back to the house, crying, "*Usga'së`ti'yu! Usga'së`ti'yu!*"

Tsul`kälû' was terribly angry. He untwisted himself and came out of the *âsï*, and said good-bye to the girl, telling her that he would never let her mother see him again, but would go back to his own country. Then he went off in the direction of *Tsunegûñ'yï*.

Soon after he left, the girl had her monthly period. There was a very great flow of blood and the mother threw it all into the river.

One night after the girl had gone to bed in the *âsï* her husband came again to the door and said to her, "It seems you are alone."

Then he asked where the child was. She said there had been none. Then he asked where the blood was and she said her mother had thrown it into the river. She told him just where the place was and he went there and found a small worm in the water. He took it up and carried it back to the *âsï*. As he walked, it took form and began to grow until, when he reached the *âsï*, it was a baby girl.

He gave it to his wife and said, "Your mother does not like me and abuses our child, so come and let us go to my home."

The girl wanted to be with her husband, so telling her mother good-bye, she took up the child and they went off together to *Tsunegûñ'yï*.

Now, the girl had an older brother, who lived with his own wife in another settlement. When he heard that his sister was married he came to pay a visit to her and her new husband, but when he arrived at *Känuga* his mother told him his sister had taken her child and gone away. Nobody knew where. He was sorry to see his mother so lonely, so he said he would go after his sister and try to find her and bring her back.

It was easy to follow the footprints of the giant and the young man went along the trail until he came to a place where they had rested. There were tracks on the ground where a child had been lying and other marks as if a baby had been born there. He went on along the trail and came to another place where they had rested and there were tracks of a baby crawling about and another lying on the ground. He went on and came to where they had rested again and there were tracks of a child walking and another crawling about. He went on until he came where they had rested again and there were tracks of one child running and another walking.

He followed the trail along the stream into the mountains and came to the place where they had rested again and this time there were footprints of two children running all about, and the footprints can still be seen in the rock at that place. Twice again, he found where they had rested.

Then the trail led up the slope of *Tsunegûñ'yï* and he heard the sound of a drum and voices, as if people were dancing inside the mountain.

Soon he came to a cave like a doorway in the side of the mountain. The rock was steep and smooth so he could not climb it. He looked over the edge and saw the heads and shoulders of a great many people dancing inside. He saw his sister dancing among them and called to her to come out.

She turned when she heard his voice and as soon as the drumming stopped, she came out to him. She had no trouble to climb down the rock, leading her two little children by the hand. She was glad to meet her brother and talked with him a long time, but did not ask him to come inside the cave. At last, he went away without having seen her husband.

Several other times her brother came to the mountain to see his sister who met him outside. He never saw her husband. After four years passed she came one day to her mother's house and said her husband had been hunting in the woods near by and they were getting ready to start home tomorrow. If her mother and brother would come early in the morning they could see her husband. If they came too late for that, she said, they would find plenty of meat to take home.

She went back into the woods and the mother ran to tell her son. They came to the place early the next morning, but *Tsul`kälû'* and his family were already gone. On the drying poles, they found the bodies of freshly killed deer hanging as the girl had promised. There were so many they went back and told all their friends to come for them and there were enough for the whole settlement.

Still the brother wanted to see his sister and her husband, so he went again to the mountain and she came out to meet him. He asked to see her husband and this time she told him to come inside with her. They went in as through a doorway and inside he found it like a great townhouse.

They seemed to be alone, but his sister called aloud, "He wants to see you."

From the air came a voice, "You can not see me until you put on new clothing and then you can see me."

The young man said to the unseen spirit, "I am willing."

From the air came the voice again, "Go back, then and tell your people that to see me they must go into the townhouse and fast seven days. In all that time they must not come out from the townhouse or raise the war whoop and on the seventh day I shall come with new dresses for you to put on so that you can all see me."

The young man went back to *Känuga* and told the people. They all wanted to see *Tsul`kälû'*, who owned all the game in the mountains, so they went into the townhouse and began the fast. They fasted the first day, the second, and every day until the seventh all but one man from another settlement, who slipped out every night when it was dark to get something to eat and slipped in again when no one was watching.

On the morning of the seventh day the sun was just coming up in the east when they beard a great noise like the thunder of rocks rolling down the side of *Tsunegûñ'yï*. They were frightened and drew near together in the townhouse, and no one whispered.

Nearer and louder came the sound until it grew into an awful roar, and every one trembled and held his breath-all but one man, the stranger from the other settlement, who lost his senses from fear and ran out of the townhouse and shouted the war cry.

At once, the roar stopped and for some time, there was silence. Then they heard it again, but as if it where going farther away and then farther and farther, until at last it died away in the direction of *Tsunegûñ'yï*, and then all was still again. The people came out from the townhouse, but there was silence and they could see nothing but what had been seven days before.

Still the brother was not disheartened, but came again to see his sister, and she brought him into the mountain. He asked why *Tsul`kälû'* had not brought the new dresses, as he had promised.

A voice from the air said, "I came with them, but you did not obey my word, but broke the fast and raised the war cry."

The young man answered, "It was not done by our people, but by a stranger. If you will come again, we will surely do as you say."

But the voice answered, "Now you can never see me."

Then the young man could not say any more, and he went back to *Känuga*.

The Lost Settlement

When the Real People still lived in the old town of *Käna'sta* on the French Broad, two strangers who looked like Real Peoples came to the settlement and made their way into the chief's house. After the first greetings were over the chief asked them from what town they had come, thinking them from one of the western settlements.

They said, "We are of your people and our town is close at hand, but you have never seen it. Here you have wars and sickness with enemies on every side and after a while, a stronger enemy will come to take your country from you. We are always happy, and we have come to invite you to live with us in our town over there."

They pointed toward *Tsuwa'tel'da* (Pilot knob), saying, "We do not live forever and do not always find game when we go for it for the game belongs to *Tsul'kälû'*, who lives in *Tsunegûñ'yï*, but there is now war. We have peace always and need not think of danger. We go now. If your people will live with us let them fast seven days and we shall come then to take them."

Then they went away toward the west and the chief called his people together in the townhouse, held a council over the matter, and decided at last to go with the strangers. They got their entire property ready for moving, went again into the townhouse, and began their fast. They fasted six days and on the morning of the seventh, before yet the sun was high, they saw a great company coming along the trail from the west led by the two men who had stopped with the chief.

They seemed just like Real People from another settlement. After a friendly meeting they took up a part of the goods to be carried and the two parties started back together for *Tsuwa'tel'da*. There was one man from another town visiting at *Käna'sta*. He went along with the rest.

When they came to the mountain, the two guides led the way into a cave, which opened out like a great door in the side of the rock. Inside they found an open country and a town with houses ranged in two long rows from east to west. The mountain people lived in the houses on the south side. They had made ready the other houses for the new comers. Even after all the people of *Käna'sta*, with their children and belongings, had moved in there were still a large number of houses waiting ready for the next who might come. The mountain people told them that there was another town of a different people above them in the same mountain and still farther above, at the very top, lived the *Ani'-Hyûñ'tïkwälâ'skï* (the Thunders).

Now all the people of *Käna'sta* were settled in their new homes, but the man who had only been visiting with them wanted to go back to his own friends.

Some of the mountain people wanted to prevent this, but the chief said, "No; let him go if he will, and when he tells his friends they may want to come, too. There is plenty of room for all."

Then he said to the man, "Go back and tell your friends that if they want to come and live with us and be always happy, there is a place here ready and waiting for them. Others of us live in *Datsu'nalâsgûñ'yï* and in the high mountains all around and if they would rather go to any of them it is all the same. We see you wherever you go and are with you in all your dances, but you cannot see us unless you fast. If you want to see us, fast four days and we will come and talk with you. Then if you want to live with us, fast again seven days, and we will come and take you."

Then the chief led the man through the cave to the outside of the mountain and left him there. When the man looked back, he saw no cave, only the solid rock. The people of the lost settlement were never seen again. It is said they are still living in *Tsuwa'tel'da*.

Strange things happen there, so the Real People know the mountain is haunted and do not like to go near it. Some years ago, a party of hunters camped there. As they sat around their fire at suppertime they talked of the story and made rough jokes about the people of old *Käna'sta*. That night they were aroused from sleep by the noise of stones thrown at them from among the trees, but when they searched, they found no one. They were so frightened they gathered up their guns and pouches and left the place never to return.

Immortals as Protectors

Once all the warriors of a certain town were off on a hunt or at a dance in another settlement.

One old man chopping wood on the side of the ridge was surprised by a party of the enemy coming upon him. Throwing his hatchet at the nearest one, he turned running for the house to get his gun to make the best defense he could.

Coming out with the gun, he was surprised to find a large body of strange warriors driving back the enemy. It was no time for questions. He took his place with the others, fighting hard until the enemy was pressed back to the creek where they broke and retreated across the mountain.

When it was over, the old man turned to thank his new friends but found he was alone. They had disappeared as though the mountain swallowed them.

Then he knew they were the *Nûñnë'hï*, who came to help their friends, the Real People.

A Race of Spirits

Yûûññwï Tsunsdi', "Little People," live in rock caves on mountainsides.

Hardly as tall as a man's knee. They are well shaped, handsome with long hair falling almost to the ground.

Great wonder workers fond of music, they spend much of their time drumming and dancing.

They are helpful and kind-hearted.

People lost in the mountains, especially children strayed from parents, are cared for and returned home by the *Yûûññwï Tsunsdi'*.

If you listen carefully sometimes their drums are heard in lonely places in the mountains.

It is not safe to follow the sound. The Little People do not like to be disturbed. They may throw a spell over the stranger so he is bewildered and loses his way. Even if he does not get back to his settlement, he is confused for as long as he lives.

Sometimes, they come near a house at night. The people inside hear them talking, but they must not go out. In the morning, they find corn gathered or a field cleared as if a whole force of men had been at work. If anyone should go out to watch, they die.

When a hunter finds anything in the woods, such as a knife or a trinket, he must say, "Little People, I want to take this."

It may belong to them. If he does not ask their permission, they will throw stones at him as he goes home.

The Cave

A hunter in winter found tracks in the snow like the tracks of little children. He wondered how they could have come there and followed them until they led him to a cave full of Little People, young and old, men, women and children.

They took him in and were kind to him, and he was with them some time. When he left, they warned him not to tell or he would die.

He went back to the settlement where his friends were anxious to know where he had been. For a long time he refused to say. At last, he told the story. A few days later he died.

The Hunter and the Great Fish

In the old days great fish called the *Däkwä'*, lived in the Tennessee River at the confluence of Toco Creek. The *Däkwä'* is so large that it could easily swallow a man.

Once a canoe filled with warriors was crossing over from the town to the other side of the river when the *Däkwä'* rose up under the boat and threw them all into the air. As they came down it swallowed one with a single snap of its jaws and dived with him to the bottom of the river.

As soon as the hunter came to his senses he found that he had not been hurt, but it was so hot and close inside the *Däkwä'* that he was nearly smothered. As he groped around in the dark his band struck a lot of mussel shells which the fish had swallowed. Taking one of these for a knife he began to out his way out. The fish grew uneasy at the scraping inside his stomach and came up to the top of the water for air.

The hunter kept cutting until the fish was in such pain it swam this way and that across the stream and thrashed the water into foam with its tail. Finally the hole was so large that he could look out and saw that the *Däkwä'* was now resting in shallow water near the shore. Reaching up he climbed out from the side of the fish, moving very carefully so that the *Däkwä'* would not know it.

The hunter then waded to shore and got back to the settlement, but the juices in the stomach of the great fish had scalded all the hair from his head and he was bald ever after.

Enchanted Lake

Westward from the headwaters of Oconaluftee River, in the wildest depths of the Great Smoky Mountains, between North Carolina and Tennessee, is the enchanted lake of *Atagâ'hï*, "Gall Place."

Although all the Real People know that it is there, no one has ever seen it for the way is so difficult that only the animals know how to reach it. Should a stray hunter come near the place he would know it by the whirring sound of the thousands of wild ducks flying about the lake. On reaching the spot, he would find only a dry flat without bird or animal or blade of grass, unless he first sharpened his spiritual vision by prayer and fasting and an all-night vigil.

Because it is not seen, people think the lake has dried. But one who keeps watch and fasts through the night would see it at daybreak as a wide, shallow sheet of purple water fed by springs spouting from the high cliffs around.

In the water are all kinds of fish and reptiles and swimming on the surface or flying overhead are great flocks of ducks and pigeons and all about the shores are bear tracks crossing in every direction. It is the medicine lake of the birds and animals.

Whenever hunters wound a bear, he makes his way through the woods to this lake and plunges into the water. When he comes out upon the other side, his wounds are healed. For this reason, the animals keep the lake invisible to the hunter.

Ice Man

Once upon a time, the Real People were burning the woods in the fall and the blaze set fire to a poplar tree, which continued to burn until the fire went down into the roots and burned a great hole in the ground. It burned and burned and the hole grew constantly larger. The people became frightened and were afraid it would burn the whole world. They tried to put out the fire, but it had gone too deep and they did not know what to do.

At last, some one said there was a man living in a house of ice far in the north who could put out the fire, so messengers were sent. After traveling a long distance, they came to the icehouse and found the Ice Man at home. He was a little fellow with long hair hanging down to the ground in two braided plaits.

The messengers told him their errand and he at once said, "O yes, I can help you."

He began to unplait his hair and when it was all unbraided, he took it up in one band and struck it once across his other hand and the messengers felt a wind blow against their cheeks. A second time he struck his hair across his hand and a light rain began to fall. The third time he struck his hair across his open hand there was sleet mixed with the raindrops and when he struck the fourth time great hailstones fell upon the ground, as if they had come out from the ends of his hair.

Ice Man then said, "Go back now and I shall be there to-morrow."

So the messengers returned to their people, whom they found still gathered helplessly about the great burning pit. The next day while they were all watching the fire a wind came from the north. They were afraid for they knew that it came from the Ice Man. Nevertheless, the wind only made the fire blaze up higher. Then a light rain began to fall, but the drops seemed only to make the fire hotter. Then the shower turned to a heavy rain, with sleet and hail that killed the blaze and made clouds of smoke and steam rise from the red coals.

The people fled to their homes for shelter and the storm rose to a whirlwind driving the rain into every burning crevice and piling great hailstones over the embers until the fire was dead. Even the smoke ceased. When at last it was all over and the people returned they found a lake where the burning pit had been and from below the water came a sound as of embers still crackling.

The Hunter and Corn

A hunter had been tramping over the mountains all day long without finding any game and when the sun went down, he built a fire in a hollow stump, swallowed a few mouthfuls of corn gruel and lay down to sleep, tired out and completely discouraged. About the middle of the night, he dreamed and seemed to hear the sound of beautiful singing, which continued until near daybreak and then appeared to die away into the upper air.

The next day he hunted with the same poor success and at night made his lonely camp again in the woods. He slept and the strange dream came to him again, so vividly that it seemed to him like an actual happening. Rousing before daylight, he still heard the song and feeling sure now that it was real, he went in the direction of the sound and found that it came from a single green stalk of corn (*selu*).

The plant spoke to him, and told him to cut off some of its roots and take them to his home in the settlement. The next morning he was to chew them, "go to water" before anyone else was awake, and then to go out again into the woods where he would kill many deer and from that time on would always be successful in the hunt.

The corn plant continued to talk, teaching him hunting secrets and telling him always to be generous with the game he took, until it was noon and the sun was high, when it suddenly took the form of a woman and rose gracefully into the air and was gone from sight, leaving the hunter alone in the woods.

He returned home and told his story and the people knew that he had seen *Selu*, the wife of *Kana'tï*. He did as the spirit had directed, and from that time, he was noted as the most successful of all the hunters in the settlement.

The Handsome Fairy

De'tsäätää. is a good natured fairy.

He was once a boy who ran away to the woods to avoid a scratching. He tries to keep himself invisible ever since.

He is a handsome little fellow spending his time hunting birds with blowgun and arrow.

He has many children just like him. They all have the same name.

When a flock of birds flies up suddenly as if frightened it is because *De'tsäätää* is chasing them.

He is mischievous, sometimes hiding an arrow from the bird hunter who may have shot it off into a perfectly clear space, but looks and looks without finding it.

Then the hunter says, "*De'tsäätää*, you have my arrow. If you don't give it up I'll scratch you."

When he looks again he finds it.

Fire Carrier

One spirit goes about night with a light. The Real People call it *Atsil'-dihye'gii*, "The Fire-Carrier."

They are afraid of it because they think it dangerous, although they do not know much about it.

They do not even know what it looks like, because they are afraid to stop it when they see it. It may be a *skili* instead of a spirit.

One young woman once saw the "Fire-carrier" as she was coming home at night from a trading post. It seemed to be following her. She was frightened. She whipped her horse into a run until she got away from it. She never saw it again.

Raven Mocker

Of all the Real People *skili* the most dreaded is Raven Mocker *Kââ'lanûû Ahkyeli'skï*).

It is the one that robs the dying man of life. They may be either sex. There is no sure way to know one, although they usually look withered and old because they have added so many lives to their own.

At night, when some one is sick or dying Raven Mocker goes to the place to take the life. He flies through the air in fiery shape; arms outstretched like wings, sparks trailing behind with a rushing sound like the noise of a strong wind. Every little while as he flies, he makes a cry like the cry of a raven when it dives in the air and those who hear are afraid. They know someone's life will soon end.

When Raven Mocker comes to a house he finds others of his kind waiting and unless there is a doctor on guard who knows how to drive them away they go inside. There they are invisible and frighten and torment the sick man until they kill him.

Sometimes to do this they lift him from the bed throwing him on the floor. His friends with him think he is only struggling for breath.

After the *skili* kill him, they take out his heart, eat it, adding to their own lives as many days or years they have taken from his.

No one in the room can see them. There is no scar where they take out the heart but there is no heart left in the body.

Only those who have the right medicine recognize Raven Mocker. If such a person stays in the room with the sick person the *skili* are afraid to come in. They retreat as soon as they see him because when one of them is recognized in his right shape he will die within seven days.

It is also said that when friends of a dying person

know there is no more hope they try to have medicine men stay in the house watching the body until it is buried, because after burial the *skili* do not steal the heart.

The Young Man and The Raven Mockers

While on a hunting trip, darkness fell on a young man a long way from home. There was a house near the trail where an old man and his wife lived, so the young man went to that house to sleep until morning.

There was no one home. He looked into the *ââsïï* finding no one there either. Maybe they are asleep, he thought. Maybe they have gone for water, he thought. So he stretched out in a corner to sleep.

Soon he heard a raven cry and in a little the old man came into the *ââsïï to* sit by the fire. He did not notice the young man in the dark corner.

Soon there was another raven cry outside. The old man said to himself, "Now my wife is coming."

Sure enough, an old woman came in to sit beside her husband. The young man then knew they were Raven Mockers. He was frightened and kept very quiet.

The old man said to his wife, "Well, what luck did you have?"

The old woman said, "None. There were too many doctors watching. What luck did you have?"

The old man said, "I got what I went for. There is no reason to fail, but you never have luck. Take this and cook it. Let's have something to eat."

Soon the young man smelled meat roasting. It smelled sweeter than any meat he had ever tasted. He peeped out of one eye. It looked like a man's heart roasting on a stick.

Suddenly the old woman said to her husband, "Who is over in the corner?"

The old man replied, "Nobody."

The old woman said, "Yes, there is. I hear him snoring."

She stirred the fire until it blazed lighting up the whole place. There was the young man lying in the corner. He pretended to be asleep. The old man made a noise to wake him but still he pretended to sleep. Then the old man came over and shook him.

He sat up rubbing his eyes as if he had been asleep. It was near daylight and the old woman was out in the other house preparing breakfast. The young hunter could hear her crying to herself.

He asked, "Why is your wife crying?"

The old man said, "Oh, she has lost some of her friends lately. She feels lonesome."

The young hunter knew she was crying because he heard them talking.

When they went to breakfast the old man put a bowl of corn mush before him and said, "This is all we have. We have had no meat for a long time."

After breakfast, the young man started on his way home again. He had gone only a little way when the old man ran after him to give him a fine piece of beadwork.

He said, "Take this, and don't tell anybody what you heard last night, because my wife and I always quarreling that way."

The young man took the piece but when he came to the first creek, he threw it into the water and went to the settlement, where he told the story.

A party of warriors started back with him to kill the Raven Mockers. They reached the place seven days after the first night. They found the old man and his wife lying dead in the house. They set fire to it burning the witches together.

The Rescue

Tsantääwûû' was lost in the mountains at the head of Oconaluftee River.

It was winter and very cold. His friends thought he must be dead.

After sixteen days, he came back. He said the Little People found him and took him to their cave.

There, he was well treated. He was given plenty to eat except bread. This was in large loaves, but when he took them in his hand to eat, they seemed to shrink into small cakes so light and crumbly that though he might eat all day he would not be satisfied.

After he was rested, they brought him part of the way home. When they came to a small creek, they told him to wade across to the main trail on the other side and not look back.

He waded across and turned to look back. The Little People were gone. The creek was a deep river. When he reached home, his legs were frozen to the knees. He lived only a few days.

Water Dwellers

Once upon a time before recorded time, *Yûûññwïï Amai'yïïnëë'hïï*, Water-dwellers, lived in the water and fishermen prayed to them for help.

Friendly Spirits

There are many spirits. Some are friendly. They live in people's houses. No one can see them. They protect the house preventing *skili* (bad spirit) from doing mischief.

The Sick Man

There was a man in *Tïkwäli'tsï* town who became sick. He grew worse until the doctors said he could not live. His friends went away and left him alone to die.

They were not as kind to each other in the old times as they are now because they were afraid of *skili*, the witches that came to torment dying people.

He was alone several days, unable to rise from his bed. One morning an old woman came in the door. She looked just like the other women of the settlement, but he did not know her.

She came over to the bed and said, "You are very sick. Your friends seem to have left you. Come with me, I will make you well."

The man was so near death that he could not move, but her words made him feel stronger and he asked her where she wanted him to go.

The old woman said, "We live close by. Come with me. I will show you."

He got up from his bed and followed her. She led the way down to the water. When she came to the water, she stepped in. He followed.

There was a road under the water and another country there just like that above. They went on until they came to a settlement with a great many houses. Women were going about their work. Children were playing. They met a party of hunters coming in from a hunt. Instead of deer or bear quarters hanging from their shoulders, they carried the bodies of dead men and children. Several of the bodies the man knew for those of his own friends in *Tïkwäli'tsï*.

They came to a house and the woman said, "This is where I live."

She took him in, fixed a bed for him, and made him comfortable. By this time, he was hungry and the woman knew his thoughts and said, "We must get him something to eat."

She took one of the bodies the hunters had just brought in and cut off a slice to roast. The man was terribly frightened.

She read his thoughts again and said, "I see you can not eat our food."

She turned away from him and held her hands before her stomach. When she turned around again they were full of bread and beans like those that he had at home. So it was every day, until soon he was well and strong again. Then she told him he might go home now, but he must be sure not to speak to anyone for seven days. If any of his friends should question him, he must make signs as if his throat were sore and keep silent. She went with him along the same trail to the water's edge, and the water closed over her and he went back alone to *Tĭkwäli'tsĭ*.

When he came there, his friends were surprised. They thought he had wandered off and died in the woods. They asked him where he had been. He pointed to his throat and said nothing. They thought he was not yet well and let him alone until the seven days were past. Then, he began to talk again and told them the whole story.

Mischievous Spirits

There are mischievous spirits. Two are named *Tsääwa'sïï* and *Tsääga'sïï*.

They sometimes help the hunter who prays to them.

Little *Tsääwa'sïï* is a tiny, handsome fellow. His long hair falls to his feet. He lives in grassy patches on the hillsides. He has great power over game.

To the deer hunter who prays to him he gives the skill to slip up on the deer without being seen.

It is said *Tsääga'sïï* invoked by the hunter is also very helpful, but when someone trips and falls we know *Tsääga'sïï* caused it.

Sun, Moon and Stars

The Boys

When the world was new, seven boys spent their time playing the *gatayu''sti* game, rolling a stone wheel along the ground, sliding a curved stick to strike it.

Their mothers scolded and then collected *gatayu''sti* stones, boiling them in a pot with corn for dinner.

When the boys came home hungry, their mothers dipped out the stones, saying, "Since you like the *gatayu''sti* better than the cornfield, eat stones."

The seven angry boys grumbled, "As our mothers treat us this way, let us go and never trouble them again."

They began to dance around the townhouse, praying to the spirits. At last, their mothers, afraid something was wrong, went looking for them. They saw the boys dancing around the townhouse. As they watched, the boys left the earth. With every round they danced, they rose higher and higher. The mothers ran to get their children. It was too late. The boys were above the townhouse roof.

Only one mother managed to pull her son down. He struck the ground with such force the earth closed over him.

The other six circled higher and higher. They went up the sky, where we see them now as the Pleiades, the Seven Sisters, The Big Dipper.

The Real People call it, "The Boys."

Where the Dog Ran

A corn meal thief, whipped by old women, ran howling home to the north, leaving tracks to trace his path across a darkened sky, his mouth-dropping evidence of the robbery, a white trail, a Milky Way, tracing where the dog ran.

Stars

Hunters in the night saw lights along a mountain ridge. Seeking their source they found two creatures, round bodies covered with fur, downy feathers, their small heads sticking out like the heads of terrapins. As the breeze played on the feathers showers of sparks flew.

The hunters carried the creatures to camp to take them home to the settlement.

Every night, the creatures grew brighter.

By day, they were balls of gray fur, but when the wind stirred, sparks flew.

The creatures were quiet.

No one thought they would escape.

On the seventh night, the creatures rose from the ground like balls of fire above treetops. They went higher and higher while the hunters watched and saw two bright points of light in the dark sky.

Then the hunters knew they were stars.

Some still say stars are balls of light.

Others say they are human.

Some say they are living creatures, luminous with fur or feathers.

Frog Swallows the Sun

When the sun or moon is darkened in the sky, it is because a great frog is trying to swallow it.

Everyone knows this, even the Creeks and other tribes.

And in olden times before great medicine men all died, whenever the sun darkened the Real People would come together, firing guns and beating drums to frightened the great frog who would run away and hide and the sun was all right again.

Animal Tales

Rabbit and Terrapin Race

Rabbit was a great runner.

No one thought Terrapin was anything but a slow traveler, but Terrapin was a great warrior and just as boastful as Rabbit.

The two disputed their speed. At last, they agreed to decide the matter by a race. They fixed the day, the starting place, and arranging to run across four mountain ridges. The one who came in first at the end was to be the winner.

Rabbit felt so sure he said to the Terrapin, "You know you can't run. You can never win the race, so I'll give you the first ridge. You'll have three to cross while I go over four."

Terrapin said that would be all right.

That night he went home to his family and sent for his Terrapin friends. He told them he knew he could not outrun Rabbit, but he wanted to stop Rabbit's boasting.

His friends agreed to help him.

On the day of the race all the animals were there to see the race.

Rabbit was with them.

Terrapin had gone ahead toward the first ridge as they had agreed. The animals could hardly see him because of the long grass.

Then the word was given.

Rabbit started with long jumps up the mountain. He expected to win the race before Terrapin could get down the other side.

However, before he got up the mountain he saw Terrapin go over the ridge ahead of him.

He ran on. When he reached the top, he could not see Terrapin in the long grass.

He went down the mountain and climbed the second ridge. Looking up he Terrapin going over the top of the next ridge. He was surprised and made longer jumps to catch up.

When he got to the top there was Terrapin away in front going over the third ridge.

Rabbit was getting tired and nearly out of breath, but he kept going. He went up the other ridge getting to the top just in time to see Terrapin crossing the fourth ridge to win the race.

Rabbit could not make another jump.

He fell on the ground, crying "mi, mi, mi, mi," as Rabbit does ever since when he is too tired to run.

Terrapin won the race.

The animals wondered how he could win against Rabbit. Terrapin never told. It was easy to understand, however.

Terrapin's friends looked alike. He simply posted one near the top of each ridge to wait until Rabbit came in sight and then climb over and hide in the long grass. When Rabbit came by he could not find Terrapin, so thought Terrapin was ahead.

If he had met other Terrapins, he would think it the same one because they looked so much alike.

The real Terrapin posted himself on the fourth ridge, so he came in at the end of the race, ready to answer questions if the animals suspected anything.

Because Rabbit had to lie down to rest, losing the race, the Conjurer when preparing young men for ball play boils rabbit hamstrings into soup and sends some one at night to pour it across the path along which other players come in the morning. That way the other players become tired in the same way and lose the game.

It is not always easy to do this, because the other party expects it and watchers are sent ahead to prevent it.

Rabbit Loses His Tail

When the world was young, Rabbit had a long bushy tail. It was longer and bushier than Fox's tail. Rabbit was very proud of his tail. He constantly told the other animals how beautiful his tail was.

One day Fox tired of hearing Rabbit brag about his tail. He decided to end Rabbit's boasting.

Winter came and one day it became so cold waters in the lake and streams froze. A few days later, Fox went down to the lake carrying four fish. When he got to the lake, he cut a hole in the ice. He tied the fish to his tail, then sat down waiting for Rabbit. Soon Rabbit came hopping over the ridge. Fox saw Rabbit and quickly dropped his tail into the cold water.

Rabbit hopped up to Fox saying, "What are you doing?"

"I'm fishing," answered Fox.

"With your tail?" Rabbit asked.

"Oh yes, that's the very best way to catch the most fish," Fox replied.

Rabbit said, "How long you been a fishing?"

Fox lied and said, "Oh, only about fifteen minutes."

"Have you caught any fish yet?" asked Rabbit.

Fox pulled up his tail. There were four fish hanging on it.

"What do you plan to do with the fish you catch?" asked Rabbit.

Fox said, "Well, I figure I'll fish for about a week. Then I am going to take all those fish to the Real People and trade them for beautiful tail combs. There is only one set of tail combs left and I want them."

Fox could see Rabbit was thinking.

Rabbit thought, "If I fished all night long, I would have enough fish by morning to trade to the Real Peoples.

Then I'll have those tail combs for myself."

Fox said, "It's getting late. I'm cold. I think I'll come back and fish some more in the morning."

Fox loped off over the top of the ridge.

As soon as Fox was out of sight, Rabbit dropped his tail down into the icy water. It was very cold.

However, Rabbit thought, "I want those tail combs more than anything."

Therefore, he sat down on the hole in the ice fishing all night long.

After the sun came up, Fox loped over the top of the ridge and ran up to Rabbit.

He said, "What are you doing, Rabbit?"

Rabbit's teeth chattered as he said, "Fishing."

"Have you caught any fish?" Fox asked.

Rabbit started to get up but he could not budge.

He said, "Fox, help me. I'm stuck."

Smiling, Fox walked behind Rabbit. He gave Rabbit a hard shove.

Rabbit popped out of the hole landing across the lake. His tail remained behind, stuck in the frozen water.

And that's why from that day to this, Rabbit has a short tail.

Rabbit Hunts Duck

Rabbit boasted he could do whatever he saw anyone else do. He was tricky could usually get the other animals believe it all. Once he pretended that he could swim in the water and eat fish just as Otter did. The other animals challenged him to prove it, so he fixed up a plan to deceive even Otter.

When they met again Otter said, "I eat ducks sometimes."

Said Rabbit, "I eat ducks too."

Otter challenged him to try it. They went up the river until they saw several ducks in the water and got near without being seen. Rabbit told Otter to go first. Otter never hesitated. He dived from the bank and swam under water until he reached the ducks. He pulled one down without being noticed by the others and came back in the same way. While Otter was under the water, Rabbit peeled bark from a sapling and made himself a noose.

"Now," he said, "Just watch me."

He dove in and swam a little way under the water until he was nearly choking and came up to the top to breathe. He went under again and came up again a little nearer to the ducks. He took another breath and dived under. This time he came up among the ducks and threw the noose over the head of one catching it. The duck struggled hard and finally spread its wings and flew up from the water with Rabbit hanging to the noose.

It flew on and on until at last Rabbit could not hold on. He had to let go. He had to drop. He fell into a tall, hollow sycamore stump without a hole at the bottom to get out. He stayed there until he was so hungry he had to eat his own fur. Rabbit does this ever since when he is starving. After several days, weak with hunger, he heard children playing outside around the trees.

He began to sing: "Cut a door and look at me. I'm the prettiest thing you ever did see."

The children ran home and told their father. He came and began cutting a hole in the tree.

As he chopped Rabbit inside kept singing, "Cut it larger, so you can see me better; I'm so pretty."

They made the hole larger. Rabbit told them to stand back so that they could get a good look as he came out. They stood back and the Rabbit watched his chance, jumped out and got away.

Rabbit and the Tar Wolf

A severe drought died up all the streams and lakes. Assembled in Council, the animals looked for the means to get water. It was proposed to dig a well. All agreed to do so except Rabbit. He refused because it would soil his paws. The rest dug the well finding water.

Rabbit beginning to suffer thirst. Having no right to the well He was thrown upon his wits to procure water. He determined theft was the easiest way.

The rest of the animals, surprised to find Rabbit well supplied with water, asked him where he got it. He replied that he arose early in the morning gathering dewdrops.

Wolf and Fox suspected him of theft and planned to trap him. They made a wolf of tar, placed it near the well. The following night, Rabbit came as usual to steal his supply of water. On seeing the tar wolf, he asked who was there. Receiving no answer, he repeated the demand, threatening to kick the wolf if he did not reply. Receiving no answer he kicked the wolf, stuck to the tar and was captured.

Fox and Wolf discussed what to do with him. Should they cut his head off? Rabbit protested it would be useless. It had often been tried. Other methods for killing him, were also useless he said. They decided to let him loose to perish in the thicket.

Rabbit cried out, pleading hard for his life. Wolf and Fox refused to listen. They set him loose to die in the thicket.

Out of reach of his enemies he gave a whoop, bounding away exclaiming, 'This is where I live.' "

Rabbit and Bear Dine Together

Bear invited Rabbit to dine with him. To add grease to the beans in a pot. Bear cut a slit in his side letting oil run out until they had enough to cook the dinner. Rabbit looked surprised.

He thought, "That's a handy way. I think I'll try that."

When he left he invited Bear to come to dinner four days later.

When Bear arrived Rabbit said, "I have beans for dinner, too. Now I'll get grease for them."

He drove a knife into his side. Instead of oil, blood gushed out. He fell over nearly dead. Bear picked him up, tied the wound, stopped the bleeding.

Bear scolded Rabbit, "You little fool. I'm large and strong, lined with fat all over; the knife don't hurt me. You are small and lean. You can't do such things."

Rabbit and Possum Seek Wives

Rabbit and Possum wanted a wives. However, no one would marry either of them. They talked over the matter.

Rabbit said, "We can't get wives here. Let's go to the next settlement. I'm messenger for the council. I'll tell the people I bring an order that everybody must mate at once. Then we'll be sure to get wives."

Possum thought this a good plan. They started together to the next town. As Rabbit traveled faster, he got there first. He waited outside until the people noticed him. They took him into the townhouse. When the chief asked his business Rabbit said he brought an important order from Council.

"Everyone must marry immediately."

The chief called the people together sharing the message from the council. Every animal took a mate at once. Rabbit got a wife.

Possum traveled slowly. Upon arriving, he discovered all the animals had mated. He was still without a wife.

Rabbit pretended sorry for him saying, "Never mind, I'll carry the message to the next settlement. You hurry on as fast as you can. This time you will get your wife."

Rabbit went on to the next town. Possum followed after him. When Rabbit got to the townhouse he told them the long peace made everyone lazy. So, Council declared war at once and they all began fighting right there in the townhouse. Rabbit made four great leaps getting away just as Possum arrived.

Everyone jumped on Possum, who had not thought to bring his weapons on a wedding trip. They nearly beat the life out of him. He fell over pretending to be dead until he saw a good chance to jump up and get away.

Possum never got a wife, but he remembers the lesson. Ever since he shuts his eyes pretending to be dead when cornered by a hunter.

Rabbit and Flint

In the old days, *Tawi' skala* (Flint) lived in the mountains. He helped to kill so many of them that all animals hated him. They talked of ways to rid themselves of him. However, everyone was afraid to venture near his house. Rabbit, boldest leader among them offered to go after Flint and try to kill him.

Flint was standing at his door when Rabbit came up saying, "*Siyu'*! Hello! Are you the fellow they call Flint?"

Flint answered, "Yes. That's what they call me."

Rabbit asked, "Is this where you live?"

Flint answered, "Yes; this is where I live."

Rabbit was trying to get Flint off guard. He expected Flint to invite him into the house, so he waited a while.

But when Flint made no move, Rabbit said, "Well, my name is Rabbit. I've heard a good deal about you. I came to invite you to come visit me."

Flint asked where Rabbit's house was. He told him it was down in the broom-grass field near the river. Flint promised to visit in a few days.

Rabbit said, "Why not come now and have supper with me?"

After a little coaxing, Flint agreed. They started down the mountain together.

When they came near Rabbit's hole Rabbit said, "There is my house, but in summer I generally stay outside where it is cooler."

He made a fire and they had their supper on the grass. When it was over, Flint stretched out to rest. Rabbit got some heavy sticks and a knife cutting out a mallet and wedge. Flint looked up and asked what it he was doing.

Said Rabbit, "Oh," "I like to be doing something and these may come in handy."

Flint lay down again. Soon he was sound asleep.

Rabbit spoke to him to make sure. There was no answer. He came over to Flint and with one good blow of the mallet; he drove the sharp stake into his body and ran with all his might for his own hole. Before he reached it there was a loud explosion. Pieces of flint flew all about. That is why we find flint in so many places now. One piece struck Rabbit from behind, cutting him just as he dived into his hole. He sat listening until everything seemed quiet again. Then he put his head out to look around. At that moment, another piece of Flint fell striking him on the lip, splitting it, as we still see it.

Rabbit and Wildcat Hunt Turkeys

Wildcat once caught Rabbit and was about to kill him.

Rabbit begged for his life, saying, "I'm so small I would make only a mouthful for you, but if you let me go I'll show you where you can get a whole drove of Turkeys."

Therefore, Wildcat let him up and went with him to where the Turkeys were.

When they came near the place, Rabbit said to Wildcat, "Now, you must do just as I say. Lie down as if you are dead and do not move, even if I kick you. When I give the word jump up and catch the largest one there."

Wildcat agreed and stretched out as if dead. Rabbit gathered some rotten wood and crumbled it over his eyes making them look flyblown, so that the Turkeys would think he had been dead some time.

Rabbit went over to the Turkeys and said, "Here, I've found our old enemy Wildcat, lying dead in the trail. Let's have a dance over him."

The Turkeys were very doubtful, but finally went with him to where Wildcat was lying in the road as if dead.

Rabbit had a good voice and was a great dance leader, so he said, "I'll lead the song and you dance around him."

The Turkeys thought that was fine.

Rabbit took a stick to beat time and began to sing: *"Galagi'na hasuyak', Galagi'na hasuyak'* (pick out the Gobbler, pick out the Gobbler)."

"Why do you say that?" said old Turkey. "

O, that's all right," said the Rabbit, "that's just the way he does and we sing about it."

He started the song again and the Turkeys began to dance around the Wildcat.

When they had gone around several times, Rabbit

said, "Now go up and hit him, as we do in the war dance."

So the Turkeys, thinking the Wildcat surely dead, crowded close around him and the old gobbler kicked him.

Rabbit drummed hard and sang his loudest, "Pick out the Gobbler, pick out the Gobbler."

Wildcat jumped up and caught the Gobbler.

Why Possum's Tail is Bare

Possum had a long busy tail. He was proud of it. He combed every morning and sang about it at dances. Rabbit used to have a long bushy tail too, but he lost it in a frozen lake. Therefore, Rabbit was jealous of Possum's tail. He decided to play a trick on Possum.

Council decided to hold a dance. All animals were invited to attend. They sent Rabbit to spread the news. Passing Possum's place, he asked Possum if he were coming to the dance.

Possum said, "I'll go if I have a special seat. Because I have such a handsome tail I ought to sit where everybody can see me."

Rabbit said he would see to it and send someone to comb and dress Possum's tail for the dance.

This pleased Possum.

Rabbit went to Cricket, an expert hair-cutter. The Real People call him "barber." Rabbit told Cricket to go the next morning and attend to Possum's tail for the dance.

Rabbit told Cricket exactly how he wanted Possum's tail fixed.

Early next morning, Cricket went to Possum's place. He said he came to get Possum ready for the dance. Possum stretched himself out on the floor shutting his eyes while Cricket dressed his tail. Cricket combed out the tail, wrapped a red string around it to keep the fur smooth until that night. However, as he wound string around Possum's tail, Cricket clipped off the hair close to the roots without Possum knowing it.

At the dance that night, Possum entered the townhouse. Just as Rabbit promised, the very best seat was reserved for Possum.

Possum waited for his turn to dance. When his turn came, he loosened the red string from his tail and stepped into the middle of the dance circle.

The drummers drummed. And Possum began to sing as he danced around the circle, "See my beautiful tail." Everyone shouted.

He danced around the circle again singing, "See what a fine color it has." The animals shouted again.

He danced around again, singing, "See how it sweeps the ground." The animals shouted louder.

Possum was delighted. He danced around again singing, "See how fine the fur is."

Everyone was laughing so loud Possum stopped to see what the matter was. He looked at the circle of animals. All were laughing at him. Then he looked down at his beautiful tail.

There was not a hair left on it. It was completely bare!

Possum was so embarrassed he fell over on the ground in a dead faint with a slight grin on his face, as possums do to this very day when taken by surprise.

Tadpole Lover

It is said a girl who, every day went down to the spring for water, heard a voice singing, *"Kûnu'nü tû'tsahyesï', Kûnu'nü tû'tsahyesï'*, A bullfrog will marry you, A bullfrog will marry you."

She wondered about that until one day when she came she saw sitting on a stone by the spring a bullfrog, which took the form of a young man and asked her to marry him. She consented taking it back to the house.

Although he had the shape of a man, there was an odd bullfrog look about his face. Some say he was a tadpole, who took on human shape retaining his tadpole mouth.

To conceal it he refused to eat with the family, but stood with his back to the fire with his face screwed up pretending he had a toothache.

At last, his wife grew suspicious and turning him around to the firelight, exposing the tadpole mouth.

They ridiculed him so much he left the house forever.

When they next went to the spring they heard a voice saying, *"Ste'tsï tûya'husï, Ste'tsï tûya'husï,* "Your daughter will die, Your daughter will die."

It happened soon after.

Bullfrog Lover

Once upon a time, a young man courted a girl who liked him well enough, but her mother was so much opposed to him that she would not let him come near the house.

At last, he made a trumpet from the handle of a gourd and hid himself after night near the spring until the old woman came down for water. While she was dipping up the water, he put the trumpet to his lips and grumbled out in a deep voice like a bullfrog's, *"Yañdaska'gä hûñyahu'skä, Yañdaska'gä hûñyahu'skä,* the faultfinder will die, the faultfinder will die."

The woman thought it a witch bullfrog and was so frightened she dropped her dipper and ran back to the house to tell the people. They agreed that it was a warning to her to stop interfering with her daughter's affairs, so she gave her consent and thus the young man won his wife.

Why Bullfrog's Head is Striped

It is said Bullfrog ridiculed Brass the great gambler until Brass got angry and dared Bullfrog to play the *gatayû'stï*, the wheel-and-stick game with him. Whoever lost was to be scratched on his forehead.

Brass won as he always did and the yellow stripes on Bullfrog's head show where the gambler's fingers scratched him.

It is also said Bullfrog had a Conjurer paint his head with yellow stripes to make him appear more handsome to a pretty woman he was courting.

Which one is true depends upon who tells the story.

Deer Gets Antlers

In the beginning, Deer had no horns. His head was smooth like a doe's and he was a great runner.

Rabbit was a great jumper.

The animals were curious about which could go farther in the same time. A match was arranged between the two. A pair of antlers was the prize for the winner.

They were to start together on one side of a thicket, go through it, turn and come back. The one coming out first would get the horns. On race day, all the animals gathered. The antlers at the edge of the thicket marked the starting point. Everyone admired the horns.

Rabbit said, "I don't know this country. Let me take a look through the bushes where I am to run."

The animals approved.

Rabbit went into the thicket. He was gone so long the animals suspected he must be up to one of his tricks. They sent a messenger to look for him In the middle of the thicket he found Rabbit gnawing down bushes and pulling them away until he had a road cleared nearly to the other side.

The messenger turned quietly, came back, and told the other animals.

When Rabbit came out, they accused him of cheating. He denied it, so they went into the thicket and found the cleared road.

They agreed that such a trickster had no right to enter the race at all, so they gave the antlers to Deer who was the best runner. He has worn them ever since.

They told Rabbit that since he was so fond of cutting down bushes he must do that hereafter.

He does so to this day.

Terrapin Escapes

Possum and Terrapin went together to hunt persimmons and found a tree full of ripe fruit.

Possum climbed the tree to throw down persimmons to Terrapin just as a wolf came by snapping at the persimmons.

Before Terrapin could reach the persimmons, Possum managed to throw down a large one that lodged in the wolf's throat as he jumped at it choking him to death.

"I'll take his ears for hominy spoons," said Terrapin.

He took the wolf's ears and started home with them leaving the Possum still eating persimmons up in the tree.

Terrapin came to a house and was invited to have some gruel from a jar that is always set outside the door. He sat down beside the jar dipping up the gruel with one of the wolf's ears. The people noticed and wondered about his spoon.

Satisfied he went on coming to another house where he was asked to have some more gruel. Again he dipped it up with the wolf's ear until he had enough.

Soon the news went around that Terrapin had killed a wolf and was using his ears for spoons.

The Wolves got together and followed Terrapin's trail until they caught him, making him a prisoner. Then they held a council to decide what to do with him. They agreed to boil him in a clay pot.

They brought in a pot but Terrapin laughed at it saying if they put him into the pot he would kick it to pieces.

They said they would burn him in the fire.

Terrapin laughed again saying he would put it out.

They decided to throw him into the deepest hole in the river to drown.

Terrapin begged, praying for them not to do that, but they paid no attention. They dragged him to the river and threw him in.

That was what Terrapin wanted. He dived under the water, came up on the other side and got away.

Some say when he was thrown into the river he hit a rock, breaking his back in a dozen places.

He sang a medicine song, *Gu'daye'wu, Gu'daye'wu,* I have sewn myself together, I have sewn myself together."

The pieces came together and the scars remain to this day.

Katydid's Warning

Two hunters camping in the woods were preparing supper one night when Katydid began singing near them.

One of them said sneeringly, "*Kû!* It sings and don't know it will die before the season ends."

Katydid answered, "*Kû! niwï*; O, so you say; but you need not boast. You will die before to-morrow night."

The next day the enemy surprised the hunters.

The hunter who sneered was killed.

Origin of the Bear

Long ago there was a Real People clan called the *Ani'-Tsâ'gûhï*. In one family of this clan was a boy who used to leave home and be gone all day in the mountains. After a while, he went oftener and stayed longer. At last, he would not eat in the house at all.

His parents scolded, but it did no good and the boy still went every day until they noticed that long brown hair was beginning to grow out all over his body. They asked him why he wanted to be so much in the woods that he would not even eat at home.

Said the boy, "I find plenty to eat there and it is better than the corn and beans we have in the settlements. Pretty soon I am going into the woods to stay all the time."

His parents were worried and begged him not to leave them.

He said, "It is better there than here, and you see I am beginning to be different already, so that I can not live here any longer. If you will come with me, there is plenty for all of us and you will never have to work for it; but if you want to come you must first fast seven days."

The father and mother talked it over and then told the headmen of the clan. They held council about the matter and after everything had been said they decided: "Here we must work hard and have not always enough. There he says there is always plenty without work. We will go with him."

So they fasted seven days and on the seventh morning all the *Ani'-Tsâ'gûhï* left the settlement and started for the mountains as the boy led the way.

When the people of the other towns heard of it they were very sorry and sent their headmen to persuade the *Ani'-Tsâ'gûhï* to stay at home and not go into the woods to live. The messengers found them already on the way and were surprised to notice that their bodies were beginning to be covered with hair like that of animals, because for seven days they had not taken human food and their nature was changing.

The *Ani'-Tsâ'gûhï* would not come back.

They said, "We are going where there is always plenty to eat. Hereafter we shall be called *yânû* (bears) and when you yourselves are hungry come into the woods and call us and we shall come to give you our own flesh. You need not be afraid to kill us, for we shall live always."

Then they taught the messengers the songs with which to call them and the bear hunters have these songs still.

When they had finished the songs the *Ani'-Tsâ'gûhï* started on again and the messengers turned back to the settlements. After going a little way they looked back and saw a drove of bears going into the woods.

The first Bear Song is, "*He-e! Ani'-Tsâ'gûhï, Ani'-Tsâ'gûhï, akwandu'li e'lanti' ginûn'ti, Ani'-Tsâ'gûhï, Ani'-Tsâ'gûhï, akwandu'li e'lanti' ginûn'ti--Yû! He-e! The Ani'-Tsâ'gûhï, the Ani'-Tsâ'gûhï,* I want to lay them low on the ground, the *Ani'-Tsâ'gûhï,* the *Ani'-Tsâ'gûhï,* I want to lay them low on the ground,--*Yû!*"

The bear hunter starts out each morning fasting and does not eat until near evening. He sings this song as he leaves camp and again the next morning, but never twice the same day.

Why Mink Stinks

Mink is a great thief, so Council met to discuss the matter and decided to burn him.

They caught Mink, built a great fire and threw him into it. As the blaze went up they smelled roasted flesh. They began to think he was punished enough and would probably do better in the future. They took him out of the fire.

However, Mink was already burned black.

He remains black and whenever attacked or excited, he smells like roasted meat.

The lesson did no good.

He is still a great a thief.

Why Groundhog's Tail is Short

There was a time when seven wolves caught Groundhog.

They said, "Now we'll kill you and have something good to eat."

Groundhog said, "When we find good food we must rejoice over it as the Real People do in the Green-Corn Dance. I know you mean to kill me. I can't help my self. But, if you want to dance I'll sing for you. This is a new dance entirely. I'll lean up against seven trees in turn, you will dance out, turn and come back, as I give the signal, and at the last turn you may kill me."

The wolves were very hungry, but they wanted to learn the new dance, so they told him to go ahead.

Groundhog leaned against a tree and began the song, "*Ha'wiye'ehi.*"

The wolves danced out in front until he gave the signal, "*Yu!*" and began with *Hi'yagu'we*.

Then they turned dancing back in line.

"That's fine," said Groundhog.

He went over to the next tree and started the second song.

The Wolves danced out, turned at the signal and danced back again.

"That's very fine," said Groundhog and went over to another tree and started the third song.

The wolves danced their best and Groundhog encouraged them. At each song he took another tree and each tree was a little nearer to his hole under a stump.

At the seventh song he said, "Now, this is the last dance, When I say *Yu!* you will all turn and come after me and the one who gets me may have me."

He began the seventh song and kept it up until the wolves were away out in front. Then he gave the signal,

"*Yu!*" and made a jump for his hole.

The wolves turned and were after him, but he reached the hole first and dove in. As he got inside, a wolf caught him by the tail and gave it such a pull that it broke off.

Groundhog's tail has been short ever since.

Dog and Wolf

In the beginning, Dog was put on the mountain.
Wolf was put beside the fire.
When winter came, Dog could not stand the cold.
He came down to the settlement and drove Wolf from the fire.
Wolf ran to the mountains.
It suited him so well he prospered and increased. After a while, he ventured down to the valley killing animals in the settlements.
The Real People followed and killed him.
His brothers came from the mountains taking such revenge that ever since the Real People have feared hurting a wolf.

Why Deer's Teeth Are Blunt

Rabbit was angry. Deer had won the antlers offered as a prize in their race. Rabbit resolved to get even.

One day, soon after the race, he stretched a large grapevine across the trail and gnawed it nearly in two in the middle. Then he ran and jumped up at the vine.

He kept on running and jumping up at the vine until Deer came along and asked what he was doing.

"Don't you see?" said Rabbit.

"I'm so strong I can bite through that grapevine at one jump."

Deer could not believe this. He wanted to see it done.

Rabbit ran and made a tremendous leap biting through the vine where he gnawed it before.

Deer, when he saw that, said, "Well, I can do it if you can."

Therefore, Rabbit stretched a larger grapevine across the trail, but without gnawing it in the middle. Deer ran as he had seen Rabbit do, sprang up in the air striking the grapevine in the center. It flew back, throwing him on his head. He tried repeatedly, until he was bruised and bleeding.

"Let me see your teeth," said Rabbit.

Deer showed him his teeth, which were long like a wolf's teeth, but not very sharp.

"No wonder you can't do it," said Rabbit; "your teeth are too blunt to do anything. Let me sharpen them for you. My teeth are so sharp I can cut through a stick just like a knife."

He showed him a black locust twig, which he had shaved off in regular rabbit fashion. Deer thought it just the thing. With a hard stone Rabbit filed Deer's teeth until they were worn down almost to the gums.

"It hurts," said Deer.

Rabbit said it always hurt a little when they began to get sharp; so Deer kept quiet.

"Now try it," said Rabbit.

Deer tried again. This time he could not bite at all.

"Now you've paid for your horns," said Rabbit, jumping away through the bushes.

Ever since Deer's teeth are blunt, therefore he chews only grass and leaves.

Deer's Revenge

Deer was angry at Rabbit for filing his teeth, so he sought revenge. He pretended to be friendly until Rabbit was off his guard.

Then one day, as they were going along together talking, he challenged the Rabbit to a jumping contest. Now Rabbit is a great jumper, so he agreed.

There was a small stream beside the path in that part of the country.

Deer said, "Let's see if you can jump across this branch. We'll go back a piece, and then when I say Ku! then both run and jump."

"All right, "said Rabbit.

They got a good start and when Deer gave the word, they ran for the stream. Rabbit made one jump and landed on the other side. Deer stopped on the bank and when Rabbit looked back Deer had conjured the stream so that it was a large river.

Rabbit was never able to get back again and is still on the other side. The rabbit that we know is only a little thing that came afterwards.

Thunder and Lightning

Thunder and His Sons

Thunder and his sons live far in the west above the sky vault, where Sun goes down behind water. Rainbow is their beautiful dress.

Shamen pray to Thunder calling him Red Man because that is the brightest color of his dress.

Other Thunders live lower down in the cliffs and mountains and under waterfalls.

They travel on invisible bridges from one high peak to another where they have their town houses. The great Thunders above the sky are kind and helpful when we pray to them, but these other Thunders are always plotting mischief.

One must not point at the rainbow or the finger will swell at the lower joint.

The Man Who Loved Thunder's Sister

In the old times the people used to dance often and all night. Once there was a dance at *Sâkwi'yï*, on the Chattahoochee River. After it started two young women with beautiful long hair came in but no one knew who they were, or from where they had come.

They danced with one partner and another and in the morning slipped away before anyone knew they were gone.

However, a young warrior had fallen in love with one of the sisters because of her beautiful hair.

After the manner of the Real People he had already asked her through an old man if she would marry him and let him live with her. To this, the young woman replied her brother at home must first be consulted. The girls promised to return for the next dance seven days later with an answer.

In the meantime, if the young man really loved her he must prove his constancy by a rigid fast until then. The eager lover readily agreed and impatiently counted the days.

In seven nights, there was another dance.

The young warrior was on hand early and later in the evening, the two sisters appeared as suddenly as before. They told him their brother was willing and after the dance, they would conduct the young man to their home. Then, they warned him that if he told anyone where he went or what he saw he would surely die. He danced with them again and at daylight, the three went away just before the dance closed to avoid being followed.

The women led the way along a trail through the woods, which the young man had never noticed before. They came to a small creek, where, without hesitating, they stepped into the water.

The young man paused in surprise on the bank and thought to himself, "They are walking in the water; I don't want to do that."

The women knew his thoughts just as though he had spoken and turned and said to him, "This is not water; this is the road to our house."

He still hesitated, but they urged him on until he stepped into the water and found it was only soft grass that made a fine level trail. They went on until the trail came to a large stream, which he knew for Tallulah River. The women plunged boldly in, but again the warrior hesitated thinking to himself,

"That water is very deep and will drown me. I can't go on."

They knew his thoughts and said, "This is no water, but the main trail that goes past our house, which is now close by."

He stepped in and instead of water, there was tall waving grass that closed above his head as he followed them. They went a short distance and came to a rock cave close under Tallulah falls. The women entered. The warrior stopped at the mouth.

The women said, "This is our house. Come in and our brother will soon be home. He is coming now."

They heard low thunder in the distance. He went inside and stood close to the entrance. Then the women took off their long hair and hung it up on a rock, and both their heads were as smooth as a pumpkin.

The man thought, "It is not hair at all."

And he was more frightened than ever.

The younger woman, the one he was about to marry, sat down and told him to take a seat beside her. He looked and it was a large turtle, which raised itself up and stretched out its claws as if angry at being disturbed. The young man said it was a turtle, refusing to sit down. The woman insisted that it was a seat. Then there was a louder roll of thunder.

The woman said, "Now our brother is nearly home."

They urged him and still he refused to come nearer or sit down. Then there was a great thunderclap just behind him. Turning quickly he saw a man standing in the doorway of the cave.

The woman said, "This is my brother."

Her brother came in and sat down on the turtle, which again rose up and stretched out its claws. The young warrior still refused to come in. The brother then said that he was just about to start to a council, and invited the young man to go with him. The hunter said he was willing to go if only he had a horse. The young woman went out and soon came back leading a great *uktena* snake, that curled and twisted along the whole length of the cave. Some people say this was a white *uktena* and that the brother himself rode a red one.

The hunter was terribly frightened, and said, "That is a snake; I can't ride that."

The others insisted that it was no snake, but their riding horse.

The brother grew impatient and said to the woman,

"He may like it better if you bring him a saddle and some bracelets for his wrists and arms."

Therefore, they went out again and brought in a saddle and some armbands. The saddle was another turtle, which they fastened on the *uktena's* back, and the bracelets were living slimy snakes, which they got ready to twist around the hunter's wrists.

He was almost dead with fear, and said, "What kind of horrible place is this? I can never stay here to live with snakes and creeping things."

The brother got very angry and called him a coward and then it was as if lightening flashed from his eyes and struck the young man and a terrible crash of thunder stretched him senseless.

When at last he came to himself again he was standing with his feet in the water and both hands grasping a laurel bush that grew out from the bank, and there was no trace of the cave or the Thunder People. He was alone in the forest. He made his way out and finally reached his own settlement.

He found then that he had been gone so long that all the people thought him dead although to him it seemed only the day after the dance. His friends questioned him closely. Forgetting the warning, he told the story. In seven days, he died, for no one can come back from the underworld, tell about it, and live.

Thunder's Child

In the old times, Thunder journeyed to the east. After he returned from one of these journeys, a child was born who the People said was his son. When the boy grew up, he had sores all over his body.

His mother said to him, "Your father, Thunder, is a great doctor. He lives far in the west, but if you can find him he can cure you."

Therefore, the boy set out to find his father and be cured. He traveled westward asking every one he met where Thunder lived. At last, they told him it was only a little way ahead.

He came to the Tennessee River where lived Brass, *ÛÛññtsaiyïï,* the great gambler. Brass invented the *gatayûûstïï* game played with a stone wheel and a stick. Everyone who came that way he challenged to play against him.

The large flat rock, with the lines and grooves where they used to roll the wheel is still there with the stick turned to stone. Brass won almost every time because he was tricky. His house was filled with fine things. Sometimes he would lose.

Then he would bet all that he had, even his own life, but the winner got nothing for his trouble for Brass knew how to take on different shapes, so he always escaped.

When Brass saw the boy he asked him to stop and play a while, but the boy said he was looking for his father Thunder and had no time to play.

Brass said, "Well, he lives in the next house. You can hear him grumbling over there all the time, so we may as well have a game or two before you go on."

The boy had nothing to bet.

Brass said, "That's all right. We'll play for your pretty spots."

This made the boy angry so he said he would play, but first he had to find his father.

The news came to Thunder that a boy was looking for him claiming to be his son.

Thunder said, "I have traveled in many lands and have many children. Bring him here. We shall soon know."

When the boy arrived, Thunder told him to sit down.

Under the blanket on the seat were long, sharp thorns of honey locust the points sticking up. When the boy sat down, they did not hurt him.

Thunder knew then this was his son. He asked the boy why he had come.

"I have sores all over my body. My mother told me you were my father and a great doctor. I came to be cured."

Thunder said, "Yes, I am a great doctor. I'll soon fix you."

There was a large pot in the corner and he told his wife to fill it with water and put it over the fire. When it was boiling, he put in some roots, took the boy, and put him in the pot. He let it boil a long time.

One would think the flesh was boiled from the poor boy's bones, but then Thunder told his wife to take the pot and throw it into the river, boy and all.

She did so and ever since there is an eddy the Real People call, *"ÛÛññ'tiguhïï'*, 'Pot-in-the-water.'"

A service tree and a calico bush grow on the bank above and a great cloud of steam came up making streaks and blotches on their bark.

It has been so to this day.

When the steam cleared she saw the boy clinging to the roots of the service tree where they hung down into the water. His skin was clean. She helped him up the bank and they went back to the house.

On the way, she told him, "When we go in, your father will put a new dress on you but when he opens his box and tells you to pick out your ornaments be sure to take them from the bottom. Then he will send for his other sons to play ball against you. There is a honey-locust tree in front of the house and as soon as you begin to get tired strike at that and your father will stop the play because he does not want to lose the tree."

When they went into the house Thunder was pleased to see the boy looking so clean.

He said, "I knew I could cure those spots. Now we must dress you."

He brought out a fine suit of buckskin with belt and headdress. The boy put them on.

Thunder opened a box saying, "Now pick out your necklace and bracelets."

The boy looked and saw the box was full of all kinds of snakes gliding over each other with their heads up.

He was not afraid because he remembered what the woman told him.

He plunged his hand to the bottom, drew out a great rattlesnake, and put it around his neck for a necklace.

He put down his hand again four times, drew up four copperheads, and twisted them around his wrists and ankles.

Then his father gave him a war club saying, "Now you must play a ball game with your elder brothers. They live beyond here in the Darkening Land. I have sent for them."

He said a ball game but he meant the boy must fight for his life when the other sons came.

The other sons were older and stronger than the boy but he was not afraid and he fought them. Thunder rolled, Lightning flashed at every stroke for they were the young Thunders. The boy himself was Lightning.

At last, Lightning tired of defending against the young Thunders and aimed a blow at the honey-locust tree.

Thunder stopped the fight. He was afraid Lightning would split the tree and he saw Lightning was brave and strong.

***

Lightning told his father how Brass dared him to play and offered to play for the spots on his skin.

Thunder said, "Yes, he is a great gambler. He makes his living that way, but I will see that you win."

He brought a small gourd with a hole bored through the neck and tied it on Lightning's wrist. Inside the gourd, there was a string of beads. One end hung out from a hole in the top, but there was no end to the string inside.

Thunder said, "Now, go back the way you came, and as soon as he sees you he will want to play for the beads. He is very hard to beat, but this time he will lose every game. When he cries out for a drink, you will know he is discouraged. Strike the rock with your war club and water will come, so you can play without stopping. At the last, he will bet his life, and lose. Then send for your brothers to kill him, or he will get away."

Lightning took the gourd and his war club and started along the road by which he had come. As soon as Brass saw him, he called to him and when he saw the gourd with the bead string hanging out he wanted to play for it. Lightning drew out the string, but there seemed to be no end to it. He kept pulling until enough came out to make a circle around the playground.

Lightning said, "I will play one game against your stake. When that is over we can have another game."

They began the game with the wheel and stick. Lightning won.

Brass did not know what to think of it, but he put up another stake calling for a second game. Lightning won again.

They played until noon and Brass lost nearly everything.

It was very hot and Brass said, "I'm thirsty. I want to stop long enough to get a drink."

Lightning said, "No."

He struck a rock with his club. Water came out and they drank. They played until Brass lost his buckskins, beaded work, eagle feathers and ornaments. At last, he offered to bet his wife. They played and Lightning won her. Brass was desperate and offered to stake his life.

He said, "If I win I kill you, but if you win you may kill me."

They played. Lightning won.

Brass said, "Let me go tell my wife, so she will receive her new husband. Then you may kill me."

He went into the house, but it had two doors. Lightning waited for a long time. Brass did not come back.

When Lightning went to look for him he found Brass out the back way and was nearly out of sight going east.

Lightning ran to Thunder's house and got his brothers to help him. They brought their dog, the Horned Green Beetle, and hurried after Brass.

He ran out of sight. They followed and met an old woman making pottery and asked her if she had seen Brass.

She said, "If he came this way, he must have passed in the night for I have been here all day."

They were about to take another road when Beetle, which had been circling about in the air above the old woman made a dart at her striking her on the forehead. It rang like brass!

Then they knew it was Brass and they sprang at him.

He jumped up in his right shape running fast so he was soon out of sight again.

Beetle had struck so hard some of the brass rubbed off. We can see it on the beetle's forehead today.

They followed and came to an old man sitting by the trail carving a stone pipe.

They asked him if he had seen Brass pass and he said no, but again the Beetle, knowing Brass in any shape, struck him on the forehead so it rang like metal and the gambler jumped up in his right form and was off again before they could hold him.

He ran east until he came to the great water. Then he ran north until he came to the edge of the world and had to turn again to the west.

He took every shape to throw them off the track, but

Green Beetle always knew him and the brothers pressed him so hard that at last he could go no more and they caught him just as he reached the edge of the great western water where Sun goes to sleep.

They tied his hands and feet with grapevine, drove a long stake through his breast, and planted it far out in the deep water.

They set two crows on the end of the pole to guard it calling it *Kâagûûññ'yïï*, "Crow place."

However, Brass did not die. He cannot die until the end of the world but he lies there always with his face up.

Sometimes he struggles under the water to get free.

Sometimes the beavers, who are his friends, come and gnaw at the grapevine to release him. Then the pole shakes to scare the beavers away and the crows cry, "Kaw! Kaw! Kaw!"

Red Man

Great Thunder and his sons, the Thunder boys, live far in the west above the sky vault.

Priests pray to Thunder calling him Red Man, because that is the brightest color of his dress.

Other Thunders live lower down, in the cliffs and mountains, under waterfalls. They travel on invisible bridges between high peaks where they have their town houses.

The great Thunders above the sky are kind and helpful when we pray to them.

The Rescue of Red Man

Two brothers hunting, came to a mountain camping place. One made fire, gathering bark for shelter. The other hunted.

The hunter heard noise on top of a ridge as if two animals were fighting. He hurried through the bushes to see what it might be. He saw *Uktena* coiled around a man, choking him to death.

Fighting for his life, the man called to the hunter, "Help me, nephew. He is your enemy as well as mine."

The hunter took aim, drew the arrow to the head, sending it through *Uktena*. Blood spouted from the hole. The snake with a snap loosed its coils tumbling down the ridge into the valley, tearing up the earth like a waterspout.

The stranger stood and the hunter saw it was *Asga'ya Gi'gäägeïï*, Red Man of Lightning.

Red Man said, "You have helped me. Now I reward you. I give you medicine so you may always find game."

At dark, they went down the ridge to where the dead *Uktena* had rolled. Birds and insects had eaten the body. Only bones were left. In one place, flashes of light came from the ground.

Digging there, Red Man found an *Uktena* scale. He went to a tree struck by Lightning, gathered splinters, and made fire to burn the *Uktena* scale to a coal.

He wrapped it in deerskin, gave it to the hunter, saying, "As long as you keep this you can always kill game. But, when you go back to your camp hang the medicine on a tree outside, because it was very strong and dangerous, as all great medicine is. When you return to your cabin you will find your brother nearly dead because of the presence of *Uktena's* scale. You must take this small piece of cane I give you. Scrape a little into water; give it to your brother to drink. It will make him well again."

Red Man disappeared. The hunter could not see where he went. He returned to camp finding his brother very sick. He cured him with the cane and every day thereafter, he found game when he hunted.

The Cherokee Rose and Other Stories

The Cherokee Rose

The trail of tears was long and treacherous. Many died along the way. The Real People's hearts were heavy with sadness, their tears mingling with the trail dust.

Elders knew the survival of children depended upon the strength of women, so one evening Elders called upon Heaven Dweller.

They told Him of the Real People's suffering and tears. They were afraid the children would not survive to reach the Territory where they could rebuild the Cherokee Nation.

Heaven Dweller told them, "To let you know how much I care, I will give you a sign. In the morning, tell the women to look back along the trail. Where their tears have fallen, I will cause to grow a plant that will have seven leaves for the seven clans of the Real People. The flower is a delicate five petal white rose. In the center of the blossom gold will remind the Real People of the white man's greed for gold found on Real People land. This plant will be sturdy and strong with stickers on all the stems. It will defy anything trying to destroy it."

The next morning Elders told the women to look back down the trail. There a plant was growing fast, covering the trail where they walked. As the women watched, blossoms formed and slowly opened. They forgot their sadness.

Like the plant, the women felt strong and beautiful. As the plant protected its blossoms, they knew they would have the courage and determination to protect their children who would begin a new Nation in the West.

The Suck

At the mouth of a creek on the Tennessee River below Chattanooga, is a series of dangerous whirlpools, known as "The Suck."

The Real People say this is the place where *Ûñtsaiyï'*, the gambler, lived long ago. Because of its appearance suggesting a boiling pot, they call it, "*Ûñ'tiguhï'*, "Pot-in-the-water."

They say in the old times the whirlpool were intermittent in character. Canoe men passing the spot hugged the bank, alert for signs of coming eruptions. When he water begins to revolve more rapidly, they would stop and wait until it became quiet before proceeding.

It happened once that two men, going down the river in a canoe came near the place and saw the water circling rapidly ahead of them. They pulled up to the bank to wait until it became smooth again, but the whirlpool seemed to approach them with wider and wider circles, until they were drawn into the vortex. They were thrown out of the canoe and carried down under the water. One man was seized by a great fish and never seen again.

The other was taken round and round down to the very lowest center of the whirlpool where another circle caught him and bore him outward and upward until he was finally thrown up to the surface and floated out into shallow water where he escaped to shore.

He said afterwards that when he reached the narrowest circle of the maelstrom the water opened below him and he could look down as through the roof beams of a house. There on the bottom of the river he saw a great company of people, looking up, beckoned to him to join them. However, as soon as they put up their hands to seize him the current caught him and took him out of their reach.

Man in the Stump

A man had a field of growing corn. He went out one day to see how it was ripening and climbed a tall stump to get a better view. The stump was hollow and a bear had a nest of cubs in the bottom.

The man slipped and fell down on the cubs, which set up such a squealing the old she-bear heard them and came climbing down into the stump tail first, in bear fashion.

The man caught hold of her by the hind legs and the old bear was so frightened she at once climbed out again, dragging the man, who thus got out of the stump as the bear ran away.

Strawberries

When First Man and First Woman began to quarrel, First Woman left First Man going toward *Nûñâgûñ'yï*, the Sun land in the east.

First Man followed her, but First Woman kept going, never looking behind her, until *Une''länûñ'hï*, the great Apportioner, Sun, took pity on him asking him if he was still angry with his wife. He said he was not.

Une''länûñ'hï then asked him if he would like to have her back again. He eagerly answered yes.

So *Une''länûñ'hï* caused a patch of the finest ripe huckleberries to spring up along the path in front of First Woman.

She passed it by without paying attention to them.

Farther on, Sun put a clump of blackberries, but she refused to notice these, as well.

Other fruits, one, two, and three, and then trees covered with beautiful red serviceberries were placed beside the path to tempt her.

Still she went on until suddenly she saw in front of her a patch of large ripe strawberries, the first ever known.

First Woman stooped to gather a few to eat.

As she picked them, she chanced turned her face to the west and the memory of her husband came back to her. She found herself unable to go on. She sat down, but the longer she sat the stronger became her desire for her husband.

At last, she gathered a bunch of the finest berries starting back along the path to give them to him.

He met her kindly and they went home together.

Two Old Men

Two old men went hunting.

One had an eye drawn down. He was called *Uk-kwûnägi'ta*, "Eye-drawn-down."

The other had an arm twisted out of shape. He was called *Uk-ku'suñtsûtï*, "Bent-bow-shape."

Hunting together, they killed a deer cooking the meat in a pot. The second old man dipped a piece of bread into the soup, smacked his lips as he ate it.

The first old man asked, "Is it good?"

The second old man said, "Yes, sir! It will draw down one's eye."

Thought the first old man, "He means me."

He dipped a piece of bread into the pot, smacked his lips as he tasted it.

The second old man asked, "Do you find it good?"

The first old man said, "Yes, sir! It will twist up one's arm."

Thought the second old man, "He means me."

He got very angry and struck the first old man. They fought one another over the insults until both were dead.

The Lazy Hunter

A party of warriors on a long hunting trip in the mountains traveled until they came to a good game region. There they set up a bark hut in a convenient place near the river. Every morning after breakfast, they scattered, each man hunting all day until returning at night with whatever game they had taken.

One lazy man went out alone to hunt every morning until he found a sunny slope where he would stretch out by the side of a rock and sleep until evening. He returned every evening empty-handed, but with his moccasins torn and a long story of how he hunted all day and found nothing.

This continued until one of the other hunters began to suspect something was wrong. He decided to find out why the hunter never returned with game. The next morning he followed him secretly through the woods until he saw him come into a sunny opening, where he sat down on a large rock, took off his moccasins, and began rubbing them against the rocks until he had worn holes in them. Then the lazy fellow loosened his belt, lay down beside the rock and went to sleep.

The hunter who found him set fire to the dry leaves and watched as the flame creep close to the sleeping man, who never opened his eyes. The spying hunter went back to camp and told what he had seen.

About suppertime, the lazy hunter came in with the same old story of a long day's hunt and no game.

When he had finished the others laughed, calling him, "Sleepyhead."

He insisted that he had been climbing the ridges all day showed how worn his moccasins not knowing that they were scorched by the fire, while he slept. When they saw the blackened moccasins, they laughed again. He was too astonished to defend himself. The leader of the hunters declared the liar was not fit to stay with them and he was driven from camp.

Hearts Forever Broken

Once upon a time North loved South's daughter.

Seeking marriage, a willing bride, all objections put aside for love, the two were united.

Condemned for the cold he carried, North promised to take his bride away. They traveled to the land of North where the People live in icehouses.

However, with the coming of the bride, houses began leaking. It grew warmer and warmer until finally, the People came to North, begging him to send his wife home to the South before the settlement melted.

The people said, "She came from the South. She is nourished by the South. Her nature is warm, unfit for North."

North loved his wife, so he refused to return her to the south. However, as the sun grew hotter the People became more urgent in their demands.

At last, North sent his true love South, their love forever shattered. Their hearts forever broken.

When Babies are Born

Wren is the messenger of the birds. It is curious about everything. Getting up early to spy on every house, Wren gathers news for the bird council.

When a baby is born, Wren finds out whether it is a boy or girl and reports to the bird council.

If it is a boy, the birds sing in mournful chorus, "Alas! The whistle of the arrow! My shins will burn."

Birds know when a boy grows older he will hunt them with a blowgun and roast them on a stick. However, if the baby is a girl, they are glad.

They sing, "Thanks! The sound of the pestle! At her home I shall surely scratch where she sweeps."

They know that after a while they will be able to pick up stray grains where she beats corn into meal.

When Cricket hears a girl is born, it also is glad, singing, "Thanks! I shall sing in the house where she lives. "

If it is a boy, Cricket laments, "Alas! He will shoot me! He will shoot me! He will shoot me!"

It is said because boys make little bows to shoot crickets and grasshoppers.

On the birth of a new arrival Real Peoples ask, "Is it a bow or meal sifter? Is it ball sticks or bread?"

Don't Miss These Books by Vernon Schmid

Otium Sanctum: Poems for the Journey Toward
ISBN 0-7414-3124-6
(Trade Paperback. 121 Pages. $11.95. Infinity, 2006.)

Westering: New and Selected Poems, 1974-2004
ISBN 0-7414-2661-7
(Trade Paperback. 105 Pages. $11.95. Infinity, 2005.)

Houlihans and Horse Sense
ISBN 1-4134-4468-7
(Trade Paperback. 152 Pages. $20.99. Xlibris, 2004.)

Seven Days of the Dog
ISBN 1-4010-9419-8
(Trade Paperback. 193 Pages. $20.99. Xlibris, 2003.)
ISBN 1-4134-0799-4
(Hardback. 193 Pages. $30.99. Xlibris, 2003.)

Showdown at Chalk Creek: A Novel of the Old West
ISBN 1-4134-3625-0
(Trade Paperback. 135 Pages. $20.99. Xlibris, 2003.)
(Hardback. 135 Pages. $30.99. Xlibris, 2003.)

Kissing Moctezuma's Serpent
ISBN 0-89002-365-4
Trade Paperback. 54 Pages. $12.95. Northwoods, 2003.)

Hog Killers and Other Poems
ISBN 0-89002-349-2
(Trade Paperback. 45 Pages. $13.95. Northwoods, 1999.)